Z. APOCALYPSE

PHILOMEL BOOKS AN IMPRINT OF PENGUIN GROUP (USA) INC.

FOR POPPY BRISTOW

PHILOMEL BOOKS A division of Penguin Young Readers Group. Published by The Penguin Group. Penguin Group (USA) Inc., 375 Hudson Street, New York, NY 10014, U.S.A. Penguin Group (Canada), 90 Eglinton Avenue East, Suite 700, Toronto, Ontario M4P 2Y3, Canada (a division of Pearson Penguin Canada Inc.). Penguin Books Ltd, 80 Strand, London WC2R 0RL, England. Penguin Ireland, 25 St. Stephen's Green, Dublin 2, Ireland (a division of Penguin Books Ltd). Penguin Group (Australia), 250 Camberwell Road, Camberwell, Victoria 3124, Australia (a division of Pearson Australia Group Pty Ltd). Penguin Books India Pvt Ltd, 11 Community Centre, Panchsheel Park, New Delhi—110 017, India. Penguin Group (NZ), 67 Apollo Drive, Rosedale, Auckland 0632, New Zealand (a division of Pearson New Zealand Ltd). Penguin Books (South Africa) (Pty) Ltd, 24 Sturdee Avenue, Rosebank, Johannesburg 2196, South Africa. Penguin Books Ltd, Registered Offices: 80 Strand, London WC2R 0RL, England.

Edited by Tamra Tuller. Design by Amy Wu. Text set in 11.5-point Matt Antique.

Library of Congress Cataloging-in-Publication Data is available upon request.
ISBN 978-0-399-25255-6
10 9 8 7 6 5 4 3 2 1

ACKNOWLEDGMENTS

Special thanks to all who have helped along the way with the Hunting trilogy on both sides of the Atlantic. But particularly . . .

In the USA, to Michael Green and Tamra Tuller for their patience and guidance, and to my brother-in-law Captain Denis Dallaire, USAF, for his invaluable advice on military matters.

In the UK, to Ruth Knowles and Kelly Hurst at Random House for their support and input, to my brilliant agent, Philippa Milnes-Smith, to Joel Hales Waller, an inspiration—and to Jill, Tobey and Amy, my Z. nearest and dearest.

"I do not know how the Third World War will be fought, but I can tell you what they will use in the Fourth—rocks!"

Albert Einstein

0 SEEK, LOCATE, DESTROY

The creature soared above the ocean. Her wings were long lengths of leather and rust. Her great beak was pointed like a giant's spear. She rode the thermal currents, the sun hot on her back, the salt wind cooling her belly.

There was still over an hour until the battle ahead; until then she had no orders to follow and could enjoy the freedom of flight.

Freedom . . .

The blue ocean flecked with white was a mirror to the sparsely clouded sky as the miles clicked off one by one. A crosswind kicked in, buffeting her body; she beat the great fleshy sails of her wings to increase her speed.

On and on she flew, shutting out fatigue, dead on course.

When the distance separating her from her target dipped below thirty miles her brain clicked automatically into battle mode. With a blink of her enormous eyes, she switched to infrared vision, seeking out heat traces, in case the target was submerged. Her natural senses, enhanced in ways she didn't understand, brought the scent of prey to her nostrils, the cold whirl of machinery to her ears. With a blink, she selected maximum magnification and zoomed in on the target area.

Something white and alien floated on the water. A boat.

The scent of the sea was snuffed out in the rush of data, the sun's warmth was lost as her blood temperature rose and her predator's instincts kicked in.

The first hunt-and-kill tests had been games; no one got hurt, not for real. But now playtime was over. There were three living things on board the boat; they had machines she knew could hurt her. She wondered what the machines' range would be and fought to suppress her fear.

She was not allowed to be afraid. The surgeons had hacked fear from her brain along with all other emotions—or so they thought. She might act like a machine, but if the programmers realized she could feel like an animal as well, she would be recycled—thrown to the slavering monsters in the pit . . .

I want to live, she thought.

As she closed the last few miles, her senses detected

a missile incoming. Instantly she dived to a lower altitude, streaking seaward. She saw the steel projectile hurtling toward her, locked onto her body heat.

Go faster. Evade.

Programmed strategies autoloaded, screaming at her to accelerate, to fold the great sails of her wings close to her sides so that she became a kind of missile herself, to push the air from her lungs in a long breath and then—

There was a booming hiss as she plunged into the sea. Her nostrils closed. Her lungs, emptied of air, gave her no buoyancy as she needled into the deep. The missile detonated behind her with a colossal blast that sent shock waves down to the seabed and an enormous plume of water skyward. Buffeted by the vibrations, she leveled out and held her course, approaching her target now from below. The water was like a different sky. A liquid night, close and comforting around her . . .

Seven miles and closing.

Her supersharp senses soon became aware of a new threat: a torpedo, pumping through the depths, its digital tracking systems seeking her out. Propelled by her long snaking tail, she pushed down again, passing five hundred yards below the surface, six hundred yards . . . Computers in her mind told her the torpedo's precision systems would stop working accurately below eight hundred yards—

A wave of anger damped down the data. So many facts; they smoldered, filthy and foreign in her head. *Go down deeper.* She switched to true vision, turned off her battle systems. Suddenly she was alone. The blackness all around was soothing. She could go deeper and deeper into this ocean of night and never come back—

Then the torpedo exploded and her sense of peace was torn apart. She was lost in a gale of pressure and heat. Pain stabbed from her head to her heart as the computers in her mind switched on in response, half drowning her with information. Terrified and angry, she began to beat her wings, propelling herself upward.

No more debate, no more conflict.

It was time for the kill.

She broke the surface with a terrifying screech. Her prey stood on the deck of the assault craft, soft things, the weapons they clutched no use at all. Machine guns spat noise and bullets that only bruised and made her madder. One victim she clawed with flailing talons, another she smacked overboard with the sweep of a single wing.

The last soft thing kept firing, the idiot blare of his weapon driving her desire to kill. Her jaws closed on him, and she twisted her head. His spine snapped, and the firing stopped.

She tossed the limp body into the water after the others of his kind and hesitated. The sun was starting to set. The air was cool. Besides the lap of the waves, there was silence.

Objective achieved.

She could break off now, fly out of reach, make for whatever shore lay beyond the horizon . . .

But the programmers would know she had disobeyed. They could make her whole head burn with pain. Pain hard enough to kill.

She launched herself from the bloodstained boat and began the long flight back to her hidden home. *Hide what you are,* she told herself. *Wait.* With the completion of these kill tests, the work to end the world of flesh and fur would enter its final phase.

And with the last hunting, freedom would come.

1 A VIRTUAL REALITY

I wanna go home.

Adam Adlar lay rigid on the couch as electrodes were fixed to his chest and forehead, his fists and feet. Wires trailed from the pads to a battered black console and a computer on a side table. There was little else in the meeting room: two hard-backed chairs and a desk.

You're in a military base, Adam reminded himself. *What did you expect—comfy sofas and a home cinema?*

Adam shivered as his dad crowned him with a high-tech headset and finished hooking him up to the console. He tried to focus on the kind, careworn face, the gray eyes behind the round glasses, the thinning hair and frown lines.

"It's just like playing another sim, right?" Mr. Adlar

tried to give him an encouraging smile. "Gaming—the thing you love most, the thing you do best. See if you can relax, okay?"

Adam closed his eyes, tried to think himself calmer. *Imagine you're back home in Scotland, back in your bedroom . . .* He'd done that a lot lately. His room was a small, warm space painted blue and black, bulging with books and Blu-Rays and video game boxes, a place that felt safe. Or as safe as anywhere could be after all he and his dad had been through the last year.

And now you're going to relive the horror, he thought, *see through the eyes of the monsters who almost killed you. And it's all because of your genius games architect father . . .*

Tension tugged Adam's eyes back open. "You know, Dad, there are times when I wish you'd never invented Ultra-Reality."

Mr. Adlar nodded and muttered, "Me too, Ad. Just about each minute of every day."

Adam sighed. Ultra-Reality should've been so cool: a game console that drew you so far into the action, you actually *became* the character. Thanks to Mr. Adlar's incredible invention, the Think-Send system, the only controller required was the gamer's mind—you had only to *think* what you wanted the hero to do, and he would do it. It was revolutionary.

If the big games companies had bought into the concept and funded his father's work, U-R might have changed the games market forever. Instead, broke and almost bankrupt, Mr. Adlar had been forced to take cash from a shady organization called Geneflow—whose directors had darker plans for this unique technology.

"This simulation," said Adam, trying to keep the shake from his voice. "If the United States military found it in an abandoned Geneflow base, why can't they just try it out for themselves? Why drag the two of us five thousand miles to Maryland to play it for them?"

Mr. Adlar pulled off his glasses and rubbed his eyes. "The simulation the military recovered was damaged, Ad. It wouldn't run properly. They've tried all kinds of players, but it seems no one can get the Think-Send system to work correctly." He grimaced. "No one except maybe the boy whose brain waves helped create that system, who's more compatible with the technology than anyone on Earth."

"Me," said Adam softly.

He could have laughed. The situation was like the setup for some incredible game. "A boy's father gets kidnapped by scientific terrorists making hyper-evolved dinosaurs . . . They want to use Think-Send to train and teach the creatures they've created, but Dad won't play ball. The bad guys threaten to hurt the boy—but one of the dinosaurs turns good and gets to him first. Boy and dinosaur find they think alike because Boy's personality got caught up in the system. They work together to beat the baddies. But the terrorists won't quit. They're hell-bent on making their mad plans a reality . . ."

Yeah, quite a setup. Adam swallowed hard. *Only it's not a game.*

It's all real.

He shuddered at a wash of nightmare memories: T. rexes force-evolved into *Z.* rexes, prehistoric predators at the peak of their powers . . . velociraptors with freakily human minds . . . mutated sea monsters that tore whole ships apart with teeth and claws . . .

The door opened, and Adam jumped. A slim officer walked into the room, handsome and dark-skinned. His uniform was immaculate and well tailored, so that he looked more like a movie star than a military man.

"Sorry for startling you." The man's voice was like a deep purr. "I'm Colonel Oldman, Special Activities Division. You must be the Adlar boys, fresh out of the UK. Welcome to Fort Meade."

"Thanks. I'm Bill, this is Adam," said Mr. Adlar, shaking the colonel's hand. "I'm originally from Chicago myself, only moved to Edinburgh in my twenties." He paused. "And as a well-informed American citizen, I know that the SAD is the secret paramilitary unit of the Central Intelligence Agency."

"Then you don't need me to tell you just how classified this entire operation is." Colonel Oldman put a finger to his lips as if for silence, then smiled at Adam. "So, young man. You've played sims like this before, right? Gonna get it working for us?"

Cheeks reddening, Adam nodded. "I'll try."

"That's all we ask of you, Adam. That's all we ask." Oldman watched him closely. "We hear you're a natural-born gamer, and we're kind of counting on you. See, we think there might be something important on this disk, and all the evidence in this Geneflow case points to you being the guy to show us what it is."

Mr. Adlar nodded curtly. "And this is why your people summoned us here, with barely a day to pack up and fly out?"

Oldman inclined his head in apology. "I appreciate the disruption to your lives bringing you here has caused. I only wish it hadn't been necessary. But the Geneflow threat hasn't gone away like we all hoped it would. Recent events have revealed certain . . . developments."

"Developments?" Mr. Adlar frowned. "Will you stop talking in riddles and tell us what's going on?"

"Mr. Adlar, I assure you that you and your son will soon be briefed on the situation through the proper channels." Suddenly, Oldman's manner had grown as stiff as his uniform. "Now, if Adam's been connected to the console as we requested, can we capture what he sees on the computer?"

"It's all set up." With an air of reluctance, Mr. Adlar switched on the battered U-R console. A red light glowed in its casing. Then he tapped at the computer keyboard, bringing up a window on the screen. "Ready to record sound and vision."

Adam tapped his headset and smiled nervously at his dad. "Ready to try and get you some."

Oldman crossed to the far side of the room and dimmed the lights.

For a few moments, nothing happened. Adam felt his nerves fade away with the rest of reality as the world within the console worked directly with his senses.

Suddenly the meeting room didn't exist, and he was no longer a skinny teenager, isolated and afraid. A feeling of power surged through his body; a coldness hardened his mind. Around him, everything was dark. He turned to try to take in details, and the world jerked and skipped. *Glitches in the software,* he realized dimly. *Concentrate. Be as one with this world . . .*

Adam focused hard, and his surroundings smoothed out, stretching on forever, more real than anything his human senses could understand.

Human?

Here in this world, Adam knew he was no longer human. He was more than a beast, more than a bird. A single, dominating impulse burned in his mind, driving out every other thought.

It was the impulse to kill.

In a dizzying blink, Adam's sight was dazzled by a vast orange sun, low and heavy on the horizon. He looked down to find the glimmering, rolling sea far below; with a thrill, he saw that he was airborne. In the same instant, he felt the weight of his expansive, leathery wings, felt the warm currents of air caressing his sinewy skin.

He spotted a ruined city sprawling in the distance, its details lost in the reddish haze.

A place to hunt.

He beat his wings harder, eager to reach the ruins. Soon he found that his sight was like the viewfinder on a camera; he could zoom in to get a closer look. Not that there was much to see but ash and rubble and charred, misshapen buildings. Adam's eyes darted all around, scanning for the slightest movement that would betray the presence of a survivor.

Suddenly, on the edge of his vision, a shadow flitted through the debris. He blinked and zoomed in closer—and spied a human dressed in rags, slipping and stumbling over the rocks and masonry.

Eyes fixed on his new target, Adam shifted his weight, tilted his great wings and swooped down, his body slicing through the air toward the lone figure with incredible speed. There was an open wound in the creature's leg—he could almost taste the salty blood on the wind. Violent urges swelled inside him as the programmed orders burned fiercely at the forefront of his brain.

KILL ALL SURVIVORS.

Adam felt his whole body convulse with the thrill of the hunt, the anticipation of the taking of one more life. He let out a long, guttural screech of triumph. Terrified, the human creature whirled to face him, its bruised, grimy face stricken with terror. There was nowhere for it to run.

KILL IT NOW.

Closing the last few yards, Adam splayed scythelike claws, ready to seize his victim before ripping its body in two—

No. No, don't.

What was that voice? Another human to be killed?

I can't do this. I'm Adam Adlar. Not a killer. This isn't me. IT ISN'T ME.

Adam's skull felt ready to explode. An inhuman scream burst from his lungs as the world turned red and his victim's face shattered into a million pixels . . .

2 CAUGHT IN CARNAGE

With a jolt, Adam sat bolt upright on the couch, back in the darkened meeting room, panting wildly. *It's over,* he realized. *It wasn't real.*

"Ad?" His dad tugged off the headset, tousled Adam's sweaty hair. "Are you all right?"

"Think . . . so . . ." Adam's heart slapped mushily against his ribs while his dad tore the electrodes from his clammy skin.

"What happened?" Colonel Oldman sounded cross. "Was that the end of the simulation?"

"I *made* it end," said Adam's dad tersely. "You saw how distressed Adam was. I should never have let him do it. That sim was meant for animal minds, not human."

The lights glared on again; Adam flinched, screwed up his eyes.

"It's clearly a training program for Z. beasts," Mr. Adlar went on, "honing their instincts, teaching them how best to hunt and kill people."

When Oldman spoke again, it was more quietly. "On the screen . . . were we seeing . . . some kind of *pterodactyl*?"

"Yes." Adam barely recognized the tortured croak in his throat as his own. "Dad, I *was* that thing . . . flying. I was flying."

"I'm here, Adam, it's okay."

"I wanted to kill . . . I was hunting people . . . had to kill everyone . . . everyone left."

Oldman peered down at him. "Everyone left after what?"

"I don't know," Adam said. "Something bad. Something terrible . . ."

"Easy," Mr. Adlar whispered, trying to settle Adam back down on the couch. He sighed and looked up at Oldman. "I should never have agreed to this."

"You had no choice," Oldman said softly, the assurance sounding somehow sinister. "Now, while I take this video footage to the Pentagon, I'd like you to meet with some of my colleagues on the National Security Council. They want to speak to you about Geneflow."

"Right now?" Mr. Adlar was growing exasperated. "We haven't even checked into our hotel yet."

"Bear with me, Mr. Adlar." Oldman gave him a tight smile. "Recent evidence has raised fresh questions. I just hope to God we can answer them." He turned and opened the door. "I'll have someone escort you to a car in just a few minutes. They'll drive you to DC and back again afterward."

"Back here?" Mr. Adlar said sharply. But he was talking to shadows: Oldman had gone.

Adam puffed out a breath. "Did he mean DC as in Washington, DC?"

"And National Security Council as in the men and women who advise the president of the United States of America on what to do in a national crisis." Mr. Adlar sat down on the couch beside him, looking dazed. "Nice to feel wanted, isn't it?"

Adam closed his eyes and sighed. "It's the biggest thrill of my life."

An hour later, Adam was sitting in the back of a black SUV, watching through tinted windows as the interstate clogged with cars. Judging from the overhead signs, they had to be nearing Washington, DC.

About time, Adam thought. He had been playing his 3DS for much of the journey, but the constant stopping and starting of the car through the thickening traffic was beginning to make him feel sick. Besides, he reflected, once you'd played Ultra-Reality, even the most sophisticated handheld or console felt uninspiring by comparison. It had been getting harder and harder to lose himself in game play, to shut out his problems in the real world.

And now he was on his way to confront them head-on.

They turned from Thirteenth Street onto I Street Northwest—the city was a grid of letters and numbers—and Adam counted three stately parks within six blocks. It felt like a very tidy and grown-up city; a serious place for serious people.

"Whereabouts is the meeting?" Adam asked his father, who was sitting beside him.

"The Eisenhower Executive Office Building, just west of the White House. Saw the outside on a school trip once." Mr. Adlar looked at him. "How're you doing now?"

"I'm okay. Just wondering what this new evidence is all about."

His dad considered. "We know that Geneflow has been creating living terror weapons and uploading human minds into the bodies of beasts. Perhaps now we'll find out why."

Adam nodded solemnly. "Can't believe they're using pterodactyls."

His dad shrugged. "They've reengineered T. rexes and raptors—perhaps they've experimented with flying reptiles too." He placed a hand on Adam's and squeezed. "Try not to worry."

Uh-huh. Right. Adam tried to accept the intended reassurance, but all he could feel was the clamminess in his dad's grip. *Time to change the subject.* "This traffic's a nightmare. Are we going to be late?"

Mr. Adlar checked his watch. "No, we're good. The meeting doesn't start until seven, so we still have about forty minutes."

But as the SUV turned onto Seventeenth Street, there was a thunderous explosion from somewhere ahead. Their driver swore as the car jerked to a halt, almost crashing into the vehicle in front. The traffic was gridlocked, and horns were blaring.

Then Adam realized people were getting out of their cars, pointing up at the skies or running for cover. A sick feeling rose in his stomach. "Dad, what's going on?"

"I don't know." Mr. Adlar looked grave. "Driver, do you see anything?"

The driver's reply was lost beneath another boom that rocked the entire street like an earthquake. Crowds of pedestrians swarmed past in the opposite direction, the air filling with their footfalls and terrified babble.

Adam craned his neck to look upward, following their line of sight. He saw a shadow streak overhead, like something humongous in the sky—and his heart stabbed with sudden recognition.

"Zed?" Adam gripped his seat. "Dad, I think it's Zed! Did you see?"

His dad stared up at the clouds. "Zed? Are you sure?"

"Like he was in stealth mode . . ."

Memories and emotions churned inside Adam. He

had spent a good ten days trapped in the company of Zed, the first of Geneflow's prehistoric re-creations—a true-life T. rex who had been force-evolved all the way to a Z. rex, the *Z* standing for *Zenithsaurus,* or "lizard at its highest point" in plain language.

"Geneflow cloned Zed, remember?" Mr. Adlar was staring out of his own window. "Whatever's up there, I think there's more than one . . ."

Adam squinted against the evening sunlight. Geneflow had given Zed the gift of adaptive camouflage—a chemical sweat secreted by the skin that deflected light and left the massive beasts practically invisible. A blur of brickwork as they sped past buildings, or ripples in the blue as they swooped down from the sky—these were the covert clues that a creature was coming.

And now, with horror, Adam saw a cluster of hazy shadows descending on DC. *So many . . . like an army . . .*

"Dad—" he began, but the sudden pounding smack of breaking glass drowned him out as a flying pickup truck crashed through the windows of the McDonald's opposite. Screams, panic and chaos built all around as one car mounted the sidewalk and reversed wildly, trying to get away, plowing a path through the hapless pedestrians. Adam hid his eyes and heard a strained, authoritative voice above the din of the crowd as the driver switched on the car radio and sent the volume screaming with a sudden twist on the dial.

". . . asked to avoid the area of Pennsylvania Avenue,

where reports are coming in of a series of explosions in the vicinity of the White House—"

There was a supersonic rush of air and another blast went off, in the sky this time: a defensive missile, a strike back, swiftly followed by more. For a second, an enormous black silhouette was revealed in the blazing flare of light and heat, almost like an aircraft. Half blinded, Adam struggled to make sense of the image before a haze of black smoke covered the area. A keening cry tore through the thick smoke before more explosions went off, and the throaty judder of helicopters added to the cacophony.

Everything was happening so fast. Adam realized his dad was reaching forward, shaking the driver's shoulder, shouting over the clamor and telling him to release the safety locks so they could open the doors.

We're going outside into that? Adam's instinct was to huddle down in his seat, to cover his head and hide—

The windshield exploded inward as something chrome and gleaming smashed into the SUV at high speed. *A motorbike* . . . Their driver took the deadly impact, speared by the handlebars, and his whole seat shoved backward, trapping Adam's legs. Adam screamed, more in terror than pain. The dead rattle of gunfire reverberated down the street and met with a deep, animal roar of defiance. Shaking with fear, Adam felt a pressure under his armpits and saw his dad, white-faced and desperate, straining to pull him clear.

"What do we do?" Adam clung to his father, not looking at the front of the car as he wriggled his bruised legs free and curled up helplessly on the backseat. "Dad, what?"

"I don't know what's happening. But we can't stay here." His dad wrestled the passenger door open. More and more people were swarming out of the buildings now, evacuating in blind panic. As Mr. Adlar started hauling Adam out of the SUV, he was pushed aside by the scrum of people. Adam tumbled to the ground with a gasp. Someone stepped on his hand, and another trod his face against the asphalt. He cried out, rolled under the SUV for protection. Panting for breath, he stared out at the crowd, watching for his dad's scruffy loafers to appear. "Dad! Where are you?" *He'll never find me under here . . .*

Terrified, Adam pulled himself out to the roadside and scrambled to his feet. Smoke had veiled the street, and it choked him as he tried to shout over the rattle of artillery. Eyes streaming, he climbed over the crumpled hood of the SUV and jumped up onto the roof, waving his arms wildly, praying his dad would see him.

Something else did.

A shrieking cry behind him made Adam spin around. Something slammed into him, flung him across the street. Time seemed to slow, a brick wall came rushing toward him—

Then Adam was jerked sharply upward, his ribs nearly

breaking, his dangling feet skimming the stonework. Fear almost stopped his heart. *I'm not falling,* he realized. *I'm being carried.*

For a second, Adam was back in the Geneflow simulation, soaring through a ruined landscape. *Oh, my God, this thing's got to be a pterosaur.*

And I'm clamped in its jaws.

Helpless, Adam tried to shout out as the creature carried him like an owl might carry a mouse. *This thing's going to eat me, it's going to drop me, it's—*

But then he caught sight of the true scale of the carnage below, and his panic turned to shock. The White House was in ruins. The roof was caved in. The colonnades were shattered. The immaculate lawns were churned up like World War I trenches. Adam couldn't take it in. *This can't be happening.* It all seemed unreal, like an elaborate movie effect.

Smoke or gas wreathed the ruins. The iconic fountain's waters were littered with debris and bodies. Adam picked out the hazy traces of four or five colossal beasts in stealth mode rampaging through the grounds, each as big as a bungalow. *I can sort of see them 'cause I know what I'm looking for, but those people down there . . .* Secret Service men, marines, police, Adam couldn't tell them apart from this height. But he could see they were all being killed.

A burning helicopter spiraled down from nowhere and

exploded in a tornado of flame. Adam flailed in the fierce heat, screamed as the blast revealed a hunched, enormous beast, black and reptilian. Then it blurred and turned invisible again, smashing the wreckage of the copter toward the soldiers at its feet.

Adam was almost grateful when the creature that held him darted swiftly away. But the horrifying scene played on in his memory, even as the panic-ridden streets passed dizzily far below. "What do you want?" he bellowed, clinging to his invisible captor's hard, scaly flesh. "Where are we going?"

Suddenly a wide, flat rooftop lengthened into view below him. As it rushed closer, Adam was released, tossed aside like a rag. He fell onto white concrete. Palms stinging, moaning with fear, he felt his heart rock his whole body with its wild pulse. The explosions had stopped; there were only sirens now, and the deafening race of aircraft engines as a fighter jet shot past. So shaken he could hardly move, Adam crawled on all fours toward the low parapet that ringed in the roof. But there was no fire escape, no way down.

Nowhere else to go.

Only then did Adam turn to face the thing that had caught him, feeling as he did in nightmares when the final crisis was near, the game-over moment that would rip him awake.

And then his captor became visible.

It was an angular giant the size of a light aircraft, a birdlike monster with a body as big as an elephant and a face that was little more than a vast beak, big enough to swallow him whole with room to spare. The beast's upper jaw ended in a kind of circular crest, crusted in blood. Its eyes shone black, each the size of a dinner plate. But it was the thing's wings that held him transfixed—colossal sails of scaly flesh rippling over an intricate framework of bone. Stretched out as it was, its wingspan was easily greater than a light aircraft.

Not just a pterosaur. A Z. pterosaur.

Adam let out a long, shaky breath, mesmerized by the meat-hook talons on its feet, the way its chest rose and fell and the great jaws twitched. Abruptly the creature folded its wings against its scaly flanks with machinelike precision and—*K-KLAKK!*—closed its jaws. Splayed teeth protruded top and bottom like huge spikes. The bulk of the beast's body tapered into a thick, sinewy tail—the diamond-shaped flap of skin at the end lent it the look of a rudder.

The beast was real. Impossible but real.

And, oh, my God, it could kill me in a second.

Instead the creature stared, slowly tilting its head to one side, eyes unblinking. Fixed on him.

"Can . . ." Adam's voice died. He licked his lips, tried again. "Can you understand me?"

A ghostly chittering built somewhere in the belly of the beast. Its jaws began to open.

Then suddenly the creature went into spasm. It flung its wings wide open, rearing up as if angry or afraid. One wing smashed into a brick chimney, flattening it in a storm of rubble, and a weird, keening cry erupted from its jaws.

Adam's fate seemed measured in moments as, eyes narrowed and claws raised, the pterosaur beast launched itself straight at him.

3 IN THE AFTERMATH

Adam threw his hands up in front of his face—as if that could save him. But the Z. pterosaur twisted away from him and crashed instead into the rooftop parapet, smashing it to bits. A trickle of watery blood ran from one of its eyes as it lay twitching in the rubble, gasping wildly.

It's sick, Adam thought. Despite his fear, a little sympathy stirred somewhere inside him. *Maybe it's crazy. That's why it didn't kill me.*

Whatever, I'm not sticking around.

Adam's legs felt so unsteady he could barely stand, but he skirted around the creature until he reached the door to the roof-access stairwell. It was locked. He pulled out his cell, but there was no signal; everyone in the whole of DC must be calling or being called. He heard a helicopter somewhere overhead and wondered if it might see him. The pterosaur was still twitching, one wing splayed out awkwardly, like a colossal broken umbrella. *If it wakes up and sees me . . .*

Suddenly the door in front of him burst open. Adam yelled out in shock, jumped away—

And was snatched up by his father and crushed into a hug. "Ad! Oh, my God, Adam."

"Dad!" Adam winced from the pain in his ribs and pulled away. "How'd you find me?"

"When we were separated, I went to get help. The police tried to evacuate me, then I saw you being carried through the air . . ." He trailed off, slack-jawed as he took in the giant bird creature sprawled against the canopy. "Jeez, Adam, that thing had you—?"

"Don't move!" An armed police officer, panting for breath, was covering Adam and his dad with a handgun.

Still dazed, Mr. Adlar looked set to protest when another officer pushed past the first and grabbed him, bundling him onto the ground. "Hands behind your head!"

"Get off him!" Adam pointed to the pterosaur. "It's that thing you want to point your guns at!"

The first officer was already gawking at the sprawled monstrosity. "What in the name of sweet heaven . . . ?"

"I don't believe it." The second cop backed away, horrified. "This is crazy. This can't be happening."

"It just did. Deal with it." Mr. Adlar got up shakily. "What happened to that thing, Ad?"

"I don't know," Adam murmured. "It picked me up, flew over the White House, brought me here and just . . . threw a fit." He swallowed hard. "D'you think it's going to die?"

Mr. Adlar shook his head. "I have no idea."

The second officer couldn't stop staring at the creature. "What . . . what are we supposed to do?"

His question hung in the air. Adam wondered if anyone in the world had the answer.

As the numb hours rushed past, Adam felt like the whole of DC: a shell-shocked mess. Unsurprisingly, their reason for being in town—the meeting at the Eisenhower Executive building—was a write-off, since the area had been evacuated in the wake of what the media had dubbed the "White House Incident."

As the time inched toward eleven, Adam and his father were waiting in a temporary shelter set up in one of the city's many Metro stations. Colonel Oldman had at least alerted the authorities that the Adlars were not to be processed like regular witnesses and evacuees; they were to be detained "comfortably" until someone in charge got around to them. At least that meant Adam got to sit in a creaky chair in the back of a small office. Hundreds of people were crowded together on the platforms in the cavernous station, bewildered and hungry, waiting to get home.

Home. Adam kept trying to imagine his safe, warm bedroom, but his thoughts wouldn't shift from the thing that had taken him. The darkness in its eyes . . . the horrific ruins of the White House . . .

Speculation had quickly mounted that the president of the United States had not been evacuated in time, that he'd been killed—assassinated. And so he'd swiftly appeared on television in a brief press conference, condemning the "cowardly" terror attack, promising harsh retribution once the perpetrators were unmasked, lamenting the hundreds of lives lost but refusing to comment on the nature of the attack. So far, the word *dinosaur* or *pterosaur* hadn't featured in a single news bulletin; the Z. beasts' camouflage powers had cloaked them well, and Adam supposed the two cops had been sworn to secrecy.

But the president knows what really happened, thought Adam. *He's keeping quiet to stop a mass panic.*

While volunteers fielded frantic phone calls in the next room, Mr. Adlar paced pointlessly about. "Come on," he muttered. "They can't just abandon us like this."

But then Adam spied a familiar white-haired figure pushing inside the office, his portly frame swamped in scarves and overcoats. "Dad, it's Dr. Marrs!" Adam jumped up, astounded. "We haven't seen him since Raptor Island. What's he doing here?"

"Ah! Bill, Adam, I've found you at last." The old man bustled over and shook hands with them both, eyes bright as a bird's. "I'm so glad you're all right."

"I wasn't expecting the chairman of the International Science and Ethics Association to be our chauffeur tonight," Mr. Adlar said wryly. "What brings you here, Jeremy?"

"These last few months, I've been acting as a special government adviser on the Geneflow case." Marrs's English accent was rich and sharp enough to scratch diamond. "Compiling evidence, don't you know. Now, come with me. Official transport's waiting outside."

Mr. Adlar hesitated. "Last time we got into 'official transport,' Adam was nearly killed. A pterodactyl—"

"No, no, no." Marrs ushered them out through the office door and along to a lift. "*Pterodactylus* was a much smaller flying reptile." He selected the button for the top floor, the eighth. "The creature that took Adam for a ride—incidentally, we have the beast now in military custody—seems to have been evolved from *Ornithocheirus*, a pterosaur from the Cretaceous period, say, a hundred and ten million years ago. Although the tail would appear to owe more to *Rhamphorynchus* from the Jurassic—"

Mr. Adlar threw his arms up in the air. "What does it matter what the thing is called?"

"Well," said Marrs calmly, "it matters if you consider Geneflow has previously only succeeded in developing

DNA taken from reptiles like the T. rex or velociraptor, who lived around forty million years later . . ."

Adam didn't get it, but Mr. Adlar's mood seemed to darken with the realization. "They're getting results from older DNA. Their techniques are growing more advanced."

"And more diverse," Marrs agreed. "Still, it's good news that we've captured a living specimen. The other Z. beasts involved in the attack got clean away." The elevator slowed to a stop at the top floor, the doors chimed open, and Marrs stepped out briskly into a dark, concrete stairwell that stretched up into shadow.

"Why are we going up to the roof?" asked Adam.

Marrs simply pushed open the door to reveal a helicopter parked incongruously on the wide, flat asphalt. Adam felt a tingle of excitement despite himself.

"See? Official transport." Marrs's face lit up with a boyish smile. "Shall we?"

Adam and his dad followed him over to the copter. "Where did they take this Orni . . . Ornitho . . ." Adam scowled. "The Z. pterosaur, where is it now? It seemed like it was really hurt."

"It won't be feeling a thing for the time being." Marrs opened the door for them. "The creature is caged and heavily sedated at a government-owned biological research center—the Patuxent Research Refuge, near Fort Meade."

"The army base where we met Colonel Oldman?" Adam queried, scrambling inside.

"Yes. He's a good chap, Oldman." Marrs encouraged Mr. Adlar inside, then bundled in beside him and closed the door.

Mr. Adlar looked balefully at Marrs. "You're not taking us to any hotel, are you?"

"You were supposed to meet with members of the National Security Council this evening. After tonight, a good number of military top brass want to sit in on that discussion too." The rotor blades hummed and whined as they began scything the air, and Marrs had to raise his voice to be heard. "We're going to the Pentagon."

The way Adam's stomach lurched wasn't entirely due to the way the helicopter swept away from the rooftop. The Pentagon was one of the most important buildings in the world—the headquarters of the United States Department of Defense. To be going there now, in the wake of all that had happened . . .

As if things weren't crazy enough already.

Adam stared down at the city. The dark grid was lit by headlights, brake lights and streetlights, an orderly swarm of fireflies. The Washington Monument pointed like a marble sword thrust up at them, and the Potomac River beside it was an artery of black. As they swept over the water, Adam recognized the vast concrete huddle of the Pentagon, a sight familiar to him from a thousand news reports. But only now did he realize that it was actually five pentagonal buildings built one inside the other, all interconnected.

Although it was close to eleven o'clock, the Pentagon's humongous parking lots north and south were choked with traffic, and lights were on at almost every window. Adam felt both sick and thrilled as the helicopter descended toward the white slab of the helipad right outside.

"It doesn't make sense," mused Dr. Marrs. "The Pentagon workspace covers almost thirty acres. Around twenty-four thousand military and civilian employees work here. It's a far greater tactical target than the White House."

"I don't think this was about tactics." Mr. Adlar looked tired and drawn in the ghostly blue light of the copter's interior. "It was about making a point. The president—the most powerful figure in the most powerful nation in the world—was shown to be defenseless."

Marrs nodded grimly as the helicopter touched down lightly and uniformed figures hurried toward them. "The question is, what or who is going to be targeted next?"

4 SHOW OF STRENGTH

Adam, his father and Dr. Marrs were led through the Pentagon's never-ending corridors by two soldiers. The old doctor clutched a battered briefcase to his chest, looking keenly all about. Intimidated by the thought of the meeting ahead, Adam kept his head down and his hands in his jeans pockets.

The building's atmosphere was edgy and intense, heavy with the smell of sweat and coffee and the frenetic squeal and chitter of computer printers. Barked commands and clipped conversation burst from offices, nagging at Adam's ears.

"Invisible monsters? Get real. This was some kind of mass hallucination . . ."

"If we hadn't literally carried the president by his armpits through the evacuation tunnel, he'd have been torn apart . . ."

"The structural integrity of the Presidential Emergency Operations Center has been compromised . . ."

"Zone P-56, from the Potomac River to downtown Washington, is the most restricted airspace in the world. And yet hostiles converge on the White House in force and the Federal Aviation Administration doesn't pick up a damned thing . . . ?"

". . . YouTube's overloaded with cell-phone footage of our men firing at nothing at all—you realize how weak this makes us look . . . ?"

". . . forced to consider the use of poison gas in a future attack, even in civilian areas . . ."

Adam shuddered. The country's military ego had taken a beating along with the White House. From every doorway, he could hear talk of target assessments, counter-attacks, retaliatory strikes.

I always wanted the world to know about Geneflow. Adam chewed his lip. *But now that it does, just what is it going to do about it?*

After walking about half a mile, Adam found himself ushered into a large conference room dominated by a huge oval table. Flat-screen TVs lined the walls like dark, square windows. There were a half-dozen plush leather chairs at one end of the table and regular seating for everyone else.

Their escorts waited impassively in the doorway, barring the way out.

Adam sighed and wished that one of those impossible, invisible monsters had been Zed, coming to his rescue. *Where are you?* he wondered. *Last seen leaving Edinburgh almost a year ago . . .*

Where did you go?

Abruptly, the escorts stood aside as a tall, bald, broad-shouldered man in an air force uniform stalked inside. His military braid and ribbons proclaimed him someone of high rank, and his stern, florid expression screamed "don't mess with me!" at all comers as other aides and officers filed in behind him to take their seats. One of them was Colonel Oldman, who nodded smartly in greeting and sat down beside the Big Cheese.

Marrs gestured that the Adlars should sit. Adam took a seat beside his dad and watched uneasily as files and recording devices were pulled from cases and placed on the table.

"For those who don't know me, I am General Winters." There was a steely Texan twang to the big man's voice. "Special security director of operations on the president's personal staff." He paused. "Tonight, a cherished symbol of our country was destroyed in an attack that, for all our reach, for all our intelligence, we never saw coming." He looked hard at the ashen faces around him. "But let me assure you, we will retaliate by crushing the terrorist scum responsible. We will not rest until this goal is achieved."

There were nods around the table and a smattering of heartfelt applause.

"Colonel Oldman," the general went on without looking up from his notes, "what's the status on the . . . *wildlife* that special ops recovered from the rooftop?"

"The creature's been comatose since capture," Oldman reported. "It's being housed over at Patuxent. We have contractors building the world's largest birdcage as I speak, and scientists lining up to test the hell out of it."

"Would those scientists include Eve Halsall?" asked Dr. Marrs.

"Dr. Halsall, the so-called beast-reader?" Mr. Adlar looked surprised. "I've read about her work in science journals but—"

"She and her team are setting up their equipment at Patuxent now," Oldman broke in. "They're experts in high-level animal communication."

"Our civilian guests are experts too," General Winters announced, his voice cold and heavy. "I'm told by Dr. Marrs that Bill Adlar and his son, Adam, have more experience with Geneflow's experimental war beasts than anyone."

Adam shifted in his seat, uncomfortable as all faces turned his way.

"That is correct," said Dr. Marrs briskly, standing up.

Still dressed in his winter waterproofs, he cut an odd little figure. "It was the Adlars' testimony that first alerted us to the existence of Geneflow."

"I thought Geneflow was just a small-time bunch of weird-science extremists," said a female officer, stern and severe. "How'd they get the muscle to pull a stunt like this? Particularly when Colonel Oldman's report states that they've lost two of their key leaders in the last year."

"We don't know how many leaders they have," Marrs said dismissively. "Or members, for that matter. But we know for certain that Geneflow has a well-organized global network working toward a clear plan of attack."

"Using dinosaurs?" One of the officers wore a sour, disbelieving look on his lined face. "That *is* what you believe we're up against here, right? Intelligent dinosaurs?"

"It's the men and women behind the dinosaurs we need to worry about," said Oldman.

"*Dinosaur* is not a helpful label in any case." Marrs looked irritated. "And it's a mistake to think of these creatures as intelligent. The Z. beasts are force-evolved animals, programmed like machines to perform set tasks, using the Think-Send system devised by Bill Adlar here."

"That's how I became involved with Geneflow in the first place," Mr. Adlar mumbled. "I developed Think-Send for use in my gaming system, Ultra-Reality. The U-R console sends computer code directly into the brain, creating a virtual world. The player can interact with that world simply by thinking."

"But Geneflow adapted the process," Marrs added grimly. "They used it to educate and equip their prehistoric creatures with modern-day skills."

"I still don't see why they bothered to 'force-evolve' actual dinosaurs," said the female officer. "Why not start from scratch with custom-built monsters?"

"Because they lacked the know-how," Dr. Marrs explained. "By comparing genetic material from prehistoric dinosaurs and their present-day ancestors, they have studied evolution in action over seventy million years. And now that Geneflow fully understand the process, they can control it." He paused impressively. "These people possess the power to force-evolve DNA along whatever paths they choose."

General Winters looked flummoxed. "You're saying they can affect the development of living things?"

"More than that," Marrs informed him, "they can actually accelerate an animal's evolution, push brain and body to their optimum level of development."

"That's how the Z. rex was created," Mr. Adlar put in. "It was designed to be a massively powerful slave animal—a highly capable, precision-controlled, invisible agent of terror."

"And you believe that's what attacked the White House today?"

"Yes," said Adam without hesitation. Everyone looked at him. "I spent weeks with Zed—the first Z. rex, I mean. I learned how to make him out even when he was in stealth mode. Those things were, like, clones of Zed—I know it. Except maybe even bigger."

"Clones?" the woman queried. "You mean, living copies?"

"The scientists at Geneflow seem to have pioneered a powerful new cloning technique," said Marrs, warming to his subject. "DNA taken from the original creature is used to grow a new version, and the natural aging of the new version's cells are accelerated to bring it to maturity—"

"Put simply," Winters interrupted, "Geneflow can make any number of identical dinosaur twins."

"So they've bred an army," Oldman murmured.

"They did that with raptors," said Adam. "I saw actual dinosaur eggs that Josephs said were good to hatch. Those ones were destroyed in the end, but—"

"Josephs?" the female officer inquired.

"Samantha Josephs," said Oldman. "A criminal who specialized in the theft of scientific secrets, and a key director of Geneflow." He looked at Adam. "Now deceased."

"I saw her die. Right next to me." Adam looked down at the table as Mr. Adlar put a comforting hand on his shoulder. "Torn apart . . ."

"And as we all know now," Oldman continued, "as well as the Z. raptors, Geneflow has Z. dactyls too."

Marrs looked aggrieved. “That creature is not a pterodactyl, it’s—”

“Never mind the different varieties,” said Winters. “How do we kill these things?”

“First we should try to understand their purpose,” said Marrs. “After all, the Z. rexes can fly huge distances—so why bother to create Z. dactyls, hmm?”

Blank looks were swapped about the table.

“Well, now that we’ve caught one, we’re going to find out,” Oldman declared.

“Good,” said Marrs. “Because I believe tonight’s incident was a simple show of force. Geneflow’s program of scientific research is concluded, and they stand ready to make a serious impact on the world stage as the most powerful terrorist group in existence.” He surveyed the grim faces surrounding him. “I do hope the Patuxent beast can shed some light on their plans. Frankly, I don’t think we have much time left to stop them.”

5 EARLY MORNING CALL

Adam woke in a sweat. It took him a full minute to work out where he was—in an uncomfortable bed at Fort Meade air base. As he fell back shivering to his pillow, he found he was grateful for the soldiers outside, for the illusion of being safe, if nothing more.

The meeting had dragged on for ages, but once Adam and his dad had answered a stack of questions, they were allowed to leave while the conference continued and strategies were hatched. But there was no hope of a hotel—Colonel Oldman had insisted Adam and his dad stay at the army base, where they could be easily reached for their "ongoing assistance in this matter."

So here they were in special apartments reserved for

personnel and their families just arrived into the area. Not exactly the Hilton, but warm and dry at least.

Adam's thoughts soon turned to the enormous flying reptile, drugged and caged up just a couple of miles away. He shuddered; it was surely no coincidence that the only person snatched by one of Geneflow's creations was the boy who'd helped to mess up their plans twice before. But Adam remembered the look of pain in those dark eyes. The Z. dactyl hadn't looked like a programmed killer. More like an animal in distress.

Maybe it didn't take me to hurt me, he thought. *Maybe it recognized something in me and came for help.*

Or maybe I'm just crazy.

Then quiet, urgent mutterings carried to Adam from his dad's room across the landing. He checked his bedside clock; it was five thirty A.M. Since he was wide awake now, he decided to creep over and eavesdrop. Dad's door was shut, but light spilled from under it.

". . . as a programmed slave animal, Geneflow may not have bothered to grant her the power of speech. Or else the fit she suffered on the rooftop has left her mind damaged so she can't talk. Either way, if the questions were asked in the right way, it's possible she could be made to answer . . ."

There was a sudden bump as Mr. Adlar got out of bed. Adam raced lightly back to his own room. But his dad was only pacing, a sure sign he was getting stressed.

"Look, I am tired of people trying to use me and Adam as resources. Don't give me that bull about my moral duty. My moral duty is first and foremost to my son, and after what he went through yesterday, I won't have him involved in any experiments . . ."

Adam found himself crossing the landing and opening his dad's door. "What experiments?" he demanded.

Mr. Adlar froze, the mobile phone still pressed to his ear. "I'll have to call you back." Killing the call, he mustered an unconvincing smile. "Ad, what's up? You should be asleep."

"What experiments?" Adam persisted. "What do they want you to do? What do they want *me* to do?"

"Look . . . we'll discuss all that in the morning."

"It *is* the morning. I can't sleep anyway. Let's talk about it now."

Just then a loud rapping on the front door made Adam freeze. "Who's that?"

"Easy, Adam." Mr. Adlar tried to sound reassuring, but Adam could see the fear in his eyes. "We're surrounded by soldiers here."

Mr. Adlar crossed to the door, unbolted it and threw it open. Colonel Oldman stood framed in the doorway in full uniform, his silver eagles glinting in the light from the hallway. "What are you doing here?"

"You said you'd call me back," said Oldman, walking inside. "I was only in my office here—thought I'd save you the trouble. You see, Bill, my unit really does need you to work with Eve Halsall and her team on this straightaway."

"I appreciate that you're under great pressure to react after last night, but—"

"With respect, Bill, you don't appreciate the wider picture." Oldman looked grave. "Dozens of the world's best and brightest scientists, biologists and environmentalists have gone missing in recent months—some of the world's most credible experts on a broad array of subjects. We've managed to keep the whole thing hushed up in the interest of national security, but witnesses at several locations heard weird, screeching cries overhead and found huge claw marks in the area—even though no creature was seen."

Adam felt a tingle ghost down his spine. "That's got to be a Z. beast."

Mr. Adlar looked alarmed. "Then . . . that thing really was trying to kidnap you."

"There's more," Oldman went on. "In Australia, Germany, Mexico and Russia, genetic reserves have been raided."

Mr. Adlar must've noticed the blank look on Adam's face. "Genetic reserves are where animal embryos and seeds are kept preserved in cold storage," he explained, "in case of some future disaster." He looked at Oldman. "Are you sure those robberies are Geneflow's work?"

"Not only did the raiders possess the skill to bypass the highest security systems and safely remove specimens, but also the brute force required to tear steel vault doors from their hinges." Oldman nodded slowly. "And you know what they took? Mainly livestock and cereal crops—the types of cattle that give the most milk and meat, the staple food plants like rice and wheat and so on."

"I don't get it," said Adam. "Why would they do that?"

"Messing with DNA is Geneflow's thing," said Oldman. "But I can't see them making a supersized Z. cow to feed the world, can you?"

Mr. Adlar frowned. "You think they're planning to attack the world's agriculture?"

"Take away a country's ability to feed itself, and you're in a real good position to make terms," said Oldman. "If they infect the food chain with poisoned crops or livestock—"

"There could be a global disaster. Starvation, riots." Mr. Adlar looked pale. "But how does that fit with an attack on the White House?"

"We don't know," Oldman said simply. "And we *need* to know. Right now, before something big and bad kicks off. Which is why I need you—and your son—to join the team at Patuxent." He paused. "You'll be properly paid for your time and expertise, of course. Come through for us, and you'll find the rewards are generous."

Mr. Adlar chewed his lip, hesitant. "Why do you need Adam?"

"Same reason we needed him to run that simulation.

Experience." Oldman held up a hand as Mr. Adlar began to protest. "Look, I'll explain when we get there. Can we get going?"

Adam blinked. "You mean now?"

"I mean *right* now." Oldman half smiled and checked his watch. "Five minutes to get dressed, troops. Then we're out of here."

6 TO READ MINDS

Adam yawned as he and his father rode to the biological research center in Oldman's Lexus. Flags twitched on tall poles in a lazy salute as the car rolled past. Security challenged them at the main gate, but the colonel's pass got them straight inside. The road wound through open countryside, wetlands and meadows, lakes and marshes.

"How big is this place?" Adam wondered.

"Twenty square miles, give or take," Oldman informed him. "It's a wildlife refuge as well as an institute for applied environmental science. Though I'm guessing there's never been a refugee like the Z. dactyl here before."

The car pulled up outside a huge industrial unit the size of an aircraft hangar. Soldiers in gas masks stood ranged around the enormous shuttered doors, stiffening to attention as Oldman emerged from the Lexus with a briefcase. Nerves gnawed at Adam's stomach as he and his dad got out after Oldman.

He had the weird feeling he was being watched. Nervously, Adam looked all around. There was no one in sight but the soldiers, clearly surprised to be welcoming so young a visitor to the hangar.

With a shiver, Adam followed his dad and the colonel inside the building through a STAFF ONLY door, into a reception area and along a clinical white corridor. Finally they reached a door marked LABORATORY.

As Oldman opened the door, Adam expected to see a super-high-tech lab bustling with men in white coats, straight out of a sci-fi movie. Instead he saw a large, tanned, gray-haired woman in a dirty white smock sitting at a wooden desk piled high with battered black-and-white monitors that were probably clunky back in the 1960s. She didn't look up, apparently engrossed in trying to make notes, eat a sandwich, drink a cup of coffee and watch the screens all at once.

"Good morning," Oldman began. "I've brought the designer of Think-Send to meet you. Eve Halsall, this is—"

"Wait." Concentrating on one of the screens, Eve held up her sandwich to silence him. "I think Zoe's coaxing our first pictures out of Big Bird's head."

Who's Zoe? wondered Adam.

"Pictures?" Mr. Adlar stepped closer. "But how? The

brain doesn't store information as images—it only *decodes* images."

"Hey, you're good!" Eve declared with false jollity; to Adam she sounded Australian. "Now, could you be good somewhere else and let me get on?"

Oldman looked apologetically at Mr. Adlar. "Eve's been flown in from New Jersey at very short notice—"

"And is cranky as hell." Eve slurped her coffee. "So, Colonel—this is the video games guy you've been banging on about, right?"

"Cutting-edge computer systems architect Bill Adlar, yes," Oldman agreed. "And this is his son, Adam."

"Good to meet you, Eve," said Adam's dad. "Well, as good as it can be to meet anyone before six A.M. after no sleep."

Eve looked up at him at last and flashed a weary smile. "Tell me about it."

"I'd sooner you told *me* what all this is for." Mr. Adlar was eyeing the teetering lash-up. "It looks, uh . . ."

"Like a pile of junk," said Eve bluntly, sloshing down her coffee. "But it works. It allows us—me and my daughter, Zoe, I mean—to create a connection between us and the animal's mind."

Mr. Adlar frowned. "You mean . . . mind reading?"

"It's not magic," Eve said with the weary air of one who'd explained this point one or two thousand times before. "We interpret and manipulate delta and theta brain waves in order to re-create images and take information directly from the subject's brain."

"But surely," Mr. Adlar began, "the brain splits up whatever we see into information for decoding—contrast, color and so on."

"Yep." Eve nodded. "But this setup reverse engineers those brain patterns, so we can simulate the image here on the screen."

Adam could almost feel the big words whooshing over his head.

His dad came to his rescue: "Animals can't speak or use words. This equipment 'sees' what's on their minds and decodes it into information humans can understand."

Eve nodded. "Well, so long as it's hooked up to Zoe, it does."

"Where is your daughter?" asked Adam, watching as a big blob of mayo fell from Eve's sandwich and landed in her lap.

"In the hangar. With Big Bird."

Mr. Adlar reacted. "She's in there with the Z. dactyl?"

"It's perfectly safe," said Oldman. "The creature is caged up, under guard and doped to its oversized eyeballs."

"And believe me, I couldn't have stopped her if I'd tried. She's only fifteen, but she knows her own mind. The work means everything to her." Without tearing her gaze from the screen, Eve wiped the mayo with the side of her hand and then smeared it on her shoulder. "Zoe acts like a kind of conduit, a medium joining beast and equipment together. The process wouldn't work without her—she's not just a gifted animal communicator—her brain's like an extra computer in the chain, handles a lot of the imaging."

"And so takes the load off the regular computers," Mr. Adlar noted.

Oldman cleared his throat a little impatiently. "Now, since this beast either can't or won't use language in the way other Z. beasts have, I'm hoping we can interrogate her—"

"*Talk* to her," Eve broke in.

"—by using Adam to ask questions with Think-Send and getting the answers back through Zoe."

Mr. Adlar shook his head. "Why are you set on using my son like this?"

"I've had a team of men trying to communicate with that thing using the hookup you saw at the base," Oldman shot back. "They got zero response, and I don't have time to fool around—I need someone with experience of connecting to these creatures using Think-Send." He gestured to Adam. "Your son *has* that experience."

"He's right." Adam shuddered, remembering how he'd once had to direct the sea monsters surrounding Raptor Island. "You have to kind of . . . reach out to the animal. Touch its mind." He swallowed hard, looked from his dad to Oldman. "Okay. I'll give it a shot."

Oldman smiled. “Thank you.”

“Even assuming Adam can get through to the Z. dactyl”—Mr. Adlar looked doubtful—“isn’t there the risk that Zoe brings bias to the results? I mean, couldn’t it be *her* feelings these scanners pick up on and—”

“Well, let’s find out, shall we, Bill?” Eve was leaning closer to one of the screens. “Here we go. Brain pulse low down in the delta zone, two cycles per second. Resolution’s usually low, but you can see the image coming together.”

Adam looked over Eve’s shoulder as his dad and Oldman peered in behind him. The image was bleached white, black lines shading in, sketchy and flickering. Slowly, details formed. Adam thought he could make out a city skyline with clouds overhead.

And something else.

“I’ve never seen an image so clear,” Eve marveled quietly. “What we’re seeing is the overwhelming image in that animal’s mind.”

With prickly shivers Adam saw a face materializing slowly in the center of the screen, staring out at them. The hair stood on end as if windblown. The eyes were wide, and the mouth even wider . . .

“No way,” breathed Adam as the grainy details hardened.

“It’s you, Adam.” Mr. Adlar stared at the terrified face on the screen. “You, being carried over DC. That creature is picturing *you.*”

7 THE DINOSAUR WHISPERER

Why me? thought Adam, walking down the corridor toward the hangar, flanked by a guard on either side. *Why is that monster still thinking of me?*

His dad hadn't been happy at the thought of him confronting the creature, no matter how many times Oldman assured him the Z. dactyl was both securely caged as well as tranquilized to the max. But integrating Think-Send with Eve's setup was going to take time, and the colonel kept insisting that was the one thing they didn't have, which was why Adam had been dragged down here in the first place.

So while Mr. Adlar got busy with the high-tech stuff, Oldman had reluctantly allowed Adam to go see the creature before trying to reach out to it, to get used to it a little—and to see if the sight of Adam in the flesh brought any further response. *If a fifteen-year-old girl can hang out with that thing,* he thought, *so can I.*

The corridor ahead ended in a wide, heavy-duty door of corrugated metal. One of the soldiers escorting him pulled a pass card from his pocket and fed it into a reader mounted on the wall. With a low mechanical growl, the shutter rose slowly upward. Cold air wafted out from the darkness on the other side. Adam was aware his escorts were clutching their guns more tightly now.

"Big Bird's in there, kid," said the soldier with the pass card. He paused, looking troubled. "It's all right. We'll go in with you."

Adam nodded, took a deep breath. "Well, Zoe's in there. I bet she'll be glad of some company."

The two soldiers looked at each other. "Yeah," said one, "I expect she will."

Pass Card Man waved him in. Not wanting the soldiers to know how scared he was, Adam attempted a nonchalant stroll into the hangar ahead of them. A row of lockers formed a high wall to his left, so he couldn't see the whole space. It gave his eyes time to adjust. The blackness was not as absolute as he first thought; dozens of lights studded the ceiling high above, giving off the weakest of light. He felt a little more confident.

That was before he saw the Z. dactyl.

Adam felt as if he were standing on the set of some crazy monster movie. A massive cage at least half the size of the hangar had been erected, towering girders welded messily to floor and ceiling. Behind them, the colossal reptile lay on its side, wings splayed out. Its scale was breathtaking; easily twice the size of a glider, with that huge, elephant-sized body pinned down beneath a vast mesh oversized chicken wire, glowing with an eerie ultraviolet light. The long beak, as big and broad as two canoes set together, had been muzzled with steel bands. He could barely make out the head through the morass of wires and sensors placed all round it, but he saw with relief that the monster's eyes were closed. She couldn't see him for real, even if she saw him in her dreams.

"There's the dinosaur whisperer," murmured Pass Card Man. "Go ahead and say hi."

Adam suddenly noticed a figure in a chair, right in front of the bars, dwarfed by the leathery giant before her. With a quickening of his pulse, he saw the wires and cables connecting the two, leading to a stack of hard drives and monitors off to one side that lent their own flickering blue light to the weirdness of the proceedings.

Gingerly, Adam walked toward her. She had her back turned to him and was wearing a pair of strange, cobbled-together headphones so she couldn't hear him approach. He heard her mutter to herself, holding her head at an awkward angle.

But as his dim shadow fell over her, she reacted, jolting as if electrified, turning to face him. Adam jumped too.

The first thing he noticed was that the girl's neck was twisted, tilting her head toward her left shoulder. Then he saw her fingers were misshapen, and the high-back seat was actually a wheelchair. Only then, with a guilty kick, did he look at the girl's face, which was round and white and quite pretty, framed by thin red curls that she pulled on now as if to cover her neck.

"Jeez!" He saw her surprise change into embarrassment and then harden into anger. "You scared the life out of me. It's a good thing I'd just about broken the connection."

"I'm sorry," said Adam quickly. "I didn't mean to . . ."

"Okay." Zoe turned to look at her monitors, which were either dark or flatlining. "It just takes me a while to get out of the zone, that's all." She pulled a lever on the left arm of her chair and the wheels rolled backward; she was either retreating or trying to get a better look at him. "You must be Adam."

"Uh, yes. Adam Adlar," said Adam, staring at her fingers again, then trying not to. "You . . . you're Zoe, right?"

She nodded, and raised her eyebrows. "Giant prehistoric monster trapped in aircraft hangar . . . and still it's me you gawp at."

"I didn't mean to. Your mum didn't tell me you were—"

"Disabled?" Zoe's tone grew sarcastic. "Gee, I'm sorry. I can only apologize for her thoughtlessness."

"No! Sorry, that came out wrong." Adam felt himself blush and turned quickly to the Z. dactyl. "I, um . . .

wasn't looking at this thing 'cause I've seen it already. Up close." He glanced back at her. "I've been inside those jaws."

"So I saw. Inside her head." She rolled a little closer, her features softer now, but her gaze even harder. "The image our girl here shared with me. The ghost boy in her head. It's you."

"Looks like it." Adam shifted. "Now who's staring?"

"Me." Unexpectedly, she smiled. "Now that we've made each other uncomfortable, how about we shake? I'm Zoe Halsall."

"Adam Adlar." He reached out and took the offered hand.

"You can squeeze harder than that. They're tough enough." Zoe gripped his own fingers with punishing force and grinned when he yelped. "Typical whinging pom."

"Are you from Australia?"

"Stop it!" Zoe squeezed even harder. "Mum and me are from New Zealand, and don't you forget it."

Adam pulled his hand back with a cheeky smile. "I probably will. After all, Australia and New Zealand are pretty much the same place, aren't they?"

"Say that again, and I'll run you over with this chair," she countered. "Now, Scotland and England, they really are the same place . . . right?" Her smile matched his for mischief. "Where are you from, Edinburgh?"

"Spot on." Adam pushed his hands in his pockets. "You must have a good ear for accents."

"I'm just good at listening, I suppose. That's why I'm here." She shrugged. "What's your excuse? If Keera had tried chewing on me, I don't think I'd be back."

"Keera?"

"My name for her. Well, Dr. Marrs says she's been adapted from the breed *Ornithocheirus* . . ."

"You know Dr. Marrs?"

"Sure, he and Mum go way back. Science stuff, yada yada."

"And you also know how to pronounce that crazy pterosaur word."

"Or-nee-tho-KEER-as." She shrugged. "The 'keera' bit sounds best, right?"

Adam nodded. "Beats calling her Z. dactyl the whole time. Anyway, as for why I'm back, it's a long story. And since my dad and your mum are going to be ages and ages putting their gadgets and gizmos together, maybe I could tell you some of it?"

Zoe seemed to consider. "Is it going to give me nightmares?"

"If you've seen inside the heads of these creatures, you can't scare easily."

"Ha! Nothing ever came that easy to me." She turned and steered her wheelchair toward the exit. "Let's get out of here. I need some fresh air."

As he followed her, Adam glanced back over his shoulder at the captured pterosaur. One of her huge eyes had flickered open, watching him go. Dark, accusing.

And maybe, he thought, *a little afraid.*

Zoe set the pace for Adam, her electric wheelchair trundling along a track through the peaceful countryside. Normally the refuge was open to tourists, school trips, all manner of visitors. But today Patuxent was closed and the two of them had the whole wildlife reserve to themselves—aside from the entourage of soldiers assigned to make sure they stayed safe.

Adam found himself talking and talking, telling Zoe all of his terrifying adventures. How his dad had been kidnapped, how he'd wound up befriending Zed, crossing the Atlantic on the dinosaur's back, how not once but twice he'd confronted the maniacs who'd made these monsters—first in the bowels of a nuclear shelter in Edinburgh, then in a fight for survival on an island of warring raptors.

Finally he told her about his insane flight over DC the night before. She made a good audience, letting him ramble on, making all the right noises to show she was listening and interested.

"I can't believe we're talking about it so normally. You know—dinosaurs and mad scientists and stuff." Zoe shook her head. "You must've had a great view of the end of the White House, up in the air."

"It was horrible."

"Uh-huh. But maybe that's why Keera associates you with the sky. You know, she flew you all around . . ."

Zoe took a deep breath of fresh air that turned into an almighty yawn. "Sorry."

"I knew I was boring you," said Adam. Then he yawned too, and they laughed.

"I'm the one who feels boring." Zoe stopped her chair at the end of the track, looking out over a lake fringed with heather. "You've been caught up in all that crazy stuff, while I sat on my butt in New Jersey, missing Auckland, getting lousy home education and working with CIA sniffer dogs."

"Were you looking inside dogs' heads?"

"That's classified." She smiled. "Y'know, dogs love me. At least until they want to go for a run—pulling me along slows them down."

Feeling awkward, Adam tried to change the subject. "You've come from Auckland to New Jersey to Maryland. Do you always travel a lot?"

"I grease up the wheels on this chair, lasso a car's tow bar and hang on tight." Zoe smiled ruefully. "Sorry, I should let you off the hook. Uncomfortable, much? People always are." She paused. "You know, all you need to do is ask me why I look like I do, and I'll tell you."

Adam sat down on a bank of grass beside the track so he was more at her eye level. "I'm sorry. I guess I wasn't sure if you'd want to talk about it."

"Thing is, people are so busy worrying about offending me, they mostly don't talk to me at all. I weird them out, and they don't know how to handle that." She pulled her hair down over her twisted neck again, vulnerability now in her blue eyes. "It's called Proteus syndrome. It's double rare, especially in girls. Basically, some bits of your body grow too much. Out of proportion, you know? Bones, skin . . ." She shrugged, looked back out across the lake. "Sporadic overgrowth, the doctors call it. You don't want to know what *I* call it."

"It's unfair," Adam mumbled.

"Yeah, well. Is it fair that you fell into this whole mad dinosaur business, and that you've been tied up with it ever since?" Zoe shrugged. "That's just how it is. You play with the cards you're dealt, right? That's what Mum says."

"What about your dad?"

"He left. Started another family. What about your mum?"

"She died. Car accident."

Zoe screwed up her nose. "I think I liked the conversation better when there were more dinosaurs in it."

"And sniffer dogs," said Adam, forcing a smile. "Sniffer dogs are cool."

"Secret agent dogs are even cooler." Zoe smiled slyly. "Me and Mum were testing how dogs recognize their owners, how much of it is scent, how much is visual. When the CIA heard we'd got images of the dogs' owners out of their little puppy brains and onto a computer, they started thinking—"

"Send a dog out to spy for them, and no one would suspect."

"Precisely! Except then Keera showed up and we were shipped out here in one heck of a hurry."

"How did you get into this talking-to-animals stuff?" Adam wondered.

"I got the right mum." Zoe said. "She studied animal behavior and psychology at university and got kind of obsessed with the way animals can hear and see and sense stuff that we can't. And maybe it's in the genes, 'cause right from being a little kid, I found I could . . . you know, understand animals. Empathize, I guess you'd call it. Mum thought I was just playing at first, but when I knew our pet dog had something bad in her gut way before her tumor showed up, she started to get interested. Took me in after school to the lab where she works."

Adam pulled a sympathetic face. "Yeah, I've been part of that routine with my dad. Getting you involved—"

"So they don't feel so bad about spending the whole time working," Zoe concluded.

They both laughed knowingly.

"And they figure we don't know what they're doing," said Adam.

"It has been cool, though." Zoe had become confident and animated now. "I know Mum's setup looks crazy, but there's been so much tinkering with it over the years, trying to integrate my own brain waves with the translation systems . . . we're both scared to death it won't work if she ever updates it."

"Her technology has boosted what you can do naturally," said Adam. "I'll bet the military have offered to take it apart and find out exactly how it works."

"Just one or two hundred times since they got us into this," Zoe agreed. "Mum's kept them off so far." She sighed. "I hate the thought of having all this taken away from me. When Mum captures an image, or words, from inside an animal's head it's like . . . proof."

Adam thought he understood. "Proof that your mum's not crazy?"

Zoe shook her head. "Proof that I can do something most other people can't. That Zoe Halsall is more than just a medical condition. You can't believe how important that is to me." She shrugged. "I was ready to hate you for steaming in here to 'help us out.'"

Adam stiffened. "Not exactly my choice."

"I know. And if Keera didn't have so much tech in her head to keep her feelings and instincts in, I could handle her all by myself."

"I'm not trying to take anything away from you," Adam told her.

"Bit too late for that!" Her smile showed she was teasing. "I mean, you say you've actually *talked* with animals! To properly talk to something that's not human and have it talk back to you, that's awesome. Respect to you. *Awe* to you."

"It's crazy." Adam shivered. "Scary and weird. I can't tell you how weird it is."

"I did kind of notice. I mean, like, making a dinosaur wasn't impressive enough for these Geneflow guys—they had to make it speak too?"

"Right . . ." Adam paused, distracted by some distant noise of movement in the trees that bordered this part of the park. "I guess because Zed was an early experiment, able to think for himself, Geneflow thought he should be able to explain his actions." He thought of the huge animal with whom he'd shared so many frightening, desperate days and felt a pang of loneliness. Zed had protected him, tried to keep him safe before departing for who knew where. But now . . .

Wish you were here, big feller, he thought.

"You okay?" Zoe asked him.

Adam was about to nod when he heard a sudden rustling in the reeds over on the other side of the lake. The soldiers jerked into life, clicks and rattles hurled into the quiet as they cocked their weapons and took aim.

A moorhen or something flapped from out of the reeds and swam busily into the middle of the water. Zoe and Adam swapped relieved looks. Then Adam spotted further movement in the leafy brush around the lake's edge. Some shy animal was edging toward them.

The soldiers kept careful aim. Pass Card Man tossed a grin to his mate. "Fancy crispy duck for dinner tonight?"

"Not with your bullet up its crispy butt," drawled his friend, to some laughter.

Suddenly *something* broke cover, darting from the reeds and heather, making straight for the soldiers. It was moving so fast, but the world seemed to slow around Adam. The creature was small and feathered, the size of a collie but running on its hind legs. Its arms were long, its hands a mass of claws, its face sharp and toothy like a baby crocodile's. Vicious barbed hooks curled up from its ankles.

Oh, my God, it's some kind of raptor—what the—?

"Kids, get out of here!" yelled Pass Card Man, his shout drowned out by the hollow stammer of assault rifles as he and his friends opened fire. On automatic, Adam started away like a sprinter—before realizing Zoe couldn't run; she was trapped in her chair, hardly designed for speed. He stopped and turned back, saw her trundling toward him looking absolutely terrified. She couldn't see what he could see: the raptor, small but sinewy and strong, shrugging off the spray of bullets. It hurled itself into the soldiers, slashing and tearing out at their legs, bringing them down. Jaws frothing, it bit at their wrists, swiped the guns from their hands with its coiling tail.

"Come on, Zoe," Adam urged her. "Come on!"

Face and body bloodied, the raptor turned its black bright eyes to Adam and Zoe.

Then, with a gurgling hiss, it bolted toward them.

8 THE SECOND TARGET

Adam stumbled backward, terrified and defenseless, convinced he would be ripped to pieces within seconds. The raptor's pace slowed for a moment, its wild eyes darting between him and Zoe as if weighing which was the easier prey.

Then, with a sudden jerk of its body, it darted straight at the girl.

Adam watched in horror as its blood-soaked jaws clamped down on Zoe's ankle, pulling at it in a frenzied attempt to wrestle her from the wheelchair. Zoe's piercing screams jolted Adam into action, and he looked frantically around for anything that might drive off the creature.

But it was too late.

Adam screamed as loud as Zoe did as the raptor tore her leg away, shaking it wildly in its jaws. But as he stared at the severed limb in horror, Adam suddenly realized—no blood. The leg was artificial.

His sense of relief was fleeting; the creature was rapidly losing interest in the prosthetic limb and he knew it would resume its attack any second. *Got to do something.* He caught sight of the fallen soldiers by the lake, moaning and writhing in pain from their injuries. *It's okay, Zoe,* he wanted to yell bravely, *I'll draw it off!* But fear had robbed him of words. He grabbed pebbles from the muddy ground at his feet, chucked them at the raptor, then turned and pelted toward the soldiers. He sensed a sudden movement in the grass behind him as the raptor gave chase.

"Adam, no!" Zoe sounded close to tears. "It'll kill you!"

I know. God, I know. Adam snatched up Pass Card Man's fallen rifle and whirled to face his attacker, wielding the weapon like a club.

The raptor was already scuttling toward him, claws outstretched. Adam leaped back, swung the rifle butt at the beast's head with all his strength. Metal struck bone with a satisfying crack; the creature seemed momentarily stunned, a dark red trickle oozing from its jaws. He swung at it again, but this time it was too quick, dodging backward, hissing and snarling.

Adam managed a third attempt before the raptor's claws tore into the back of his hand. He cried out in pain as the rifle dropped from his bloodied fingers. "No!" he shouted helplessly as the creature readied itself to pounce.

But then more bullets pounded into its body, rounds spraying upward into its face. One eye burst open, and sharp teeth shattered. Turning in disgust, Adam saw four more soldiers racing toward them. With an angry screech, the raptor turned and bounded away at incredible speed, vanishing into the undergrowth.

Adam was still staring after it, terrified that it would double back, when the men reached him. "We heard shots fired, came running," one began. "What *was* that thing?"

"Raptor. It . . . it hurt the guards," Adam stammered.

"It hurt *you,*" the soldier noted.

Adam saw that his whole hand was covered in blood. He clutched at the dark, sticky mess, and his guts turned with nausea. "What about Zoe? It got her leg . . ."

"Don't worry. We'll check it out." Two of the soldiers pelted away.

Adam's legs could no longer support him, and he sank to his knees on the grass, his hand stinging viciously. He couldn't believe how quickly the attack had come, how close to death he'd been. *What was that raptor doing here?* he thought. *Where did it come from?*

"Easy, kid." One of the soldiers put a hand on Adam's shoulder. "We're going to get you to an ambulance, okay? You'll be all right."

Adam nodded, still staring into the undergrowth. He knew he'd survived today by chance, dumb luck.

They can get at us anytime. And anywhere.

Adam stirred slowly, crawling back into consciousness from black, dreamless sleep. As he opened his eyes, his heart began to pump—*Where am I?* Then he remembered being taken to a private room in the nearest hospital, escorted by a crowd of men in uniform. The doctor had given him something to calm him down. Since he could see by the window that it was now night, he must have gone out like a light.

The door opened suddenly, and a young soldier peered in, gun at the ready. "Heard you move. Everything okay?"

"Fine." Adam almost held his hands up—then saw that the one on the left was heavily bandaged and winced. "Uh, how long have I been sleeping?"

The soldier smiled. "Most of the day, you lazy tyke. You've got a visitor here been waiting to see you."

"Before you get too excited, it's only me." Zoe steered her wheelchair into the room, a blanket over her lap. As the soldier stepped back outside and closed the door, she watched Adam from the foot of the bed. "How are you doing? How's that hand?"

"Not so bad." Adam flexed it, winced and sat up in bed. "How are *you* doing?"

"I'm fine. The soldiers that thing attacked will be okay too, once the stitches come out."

"Did they catch it?"

"No. It vanished."

"Great. It could be anywhere." Adam shuddered. "When I saw it had your leg . . ."

Zoe looked away. "Aren't I lucky, getting one amputated when I was twelve 'cause of all that pain I was in, huh?"

"I had no idea you . . ." Adam trailed off awkwardly. "Well, I guess we owe a lot to that missing leg. It bought us time. Probably saved our lives."

"Destiny! I knew I developed this incredibly rare medical condition for a reason."

"All right, fine, I give up. Sorry." Adam slumped back crossly against his hard pillow. "I'm just trying to say thank you."

Zoe bit her lip. "I know. I try to joke about the Proteus to stop people feeling uncomfortable around me. I guess sometimes I try too hard." She looked at him. "I also find it hard to thank people, you know? Like to think I can take care of myself. But . . . thank you for leading that thing away from me. Are you okay?"

"Right now I'm not sure what I am," Adam admitted. "Have you been here for the last ten hours too?"

"Just for observation—and to be fitted for a new prosthetic. Who knows when that's going to come." She shrugged. "Anyway, since you're being guarded by half an army, Mum decided that here was the safest place for me while she works on with your dad. Oldman won't let either of them leave the lab to visit us, says it's not safe."

She paused. "You know, they think that raptor thing was gathering information. Or that maybe it attacked us because it knew we were going to try to talk with Keera—and someone didn't want that."

"Makes sense, I guess." He looked out anxiously at the night past the curtains. "But like Oldman says, we don't know *what* Geneflow's up to. How long will we be kept here, do you think?"

"That's what I came to tell you. Me and Mum are being moved into Fort Meade next to you and your dad. Oldman said he'd send a car to get us when our parents are done for the day—should be here in half an hour."

"Makes sense, I suppose," said Adam. "They can guard us all together."

Zoe nodded sullenly. "Well . . . I'll see you later, when they bring the car for us," she said. Adam got up to open the door for her, but she shook her head. With only a little difficulty, she wheeled herself parallel to the door, opened it while pushing herself backward out of its way, then glided quickly outside before it could swing shut on her.

Adam sank back against the pillow and sighed. Almost at once, he heard agitated voices from farther along the corridor:

"Oh, my God, have you seen—"

"I heard it on the news."

"CNN, quickly . . . turn it on. I don't believe it . . ."

His guts grinding with fear, Adam reached for the remote on the bedside table. As the set on the wall flickered on, he started scrolling through the unfamiliar channels, until—

The screen showed flames flaring orange and red against the black of night. The walls of some great, ornate building suddenly exploded inward amid the terrified screams of onlookers. Horrified, Adam sat up straight, trying to make sense of the footage blurring in and out of focus to a sound track of screams and gunfire. Then he saw the words scrolling along the bottom of the screen in a bloodred stripe: *London, England—The Houses of Parliament destroyed in terror strike. Hundreds believed dead. "Similar methodology to White House attack," experts claim.*

"No way." Fear clutched at Adam's throat as a blur in the air passed over the huge, imposing clock tower of Big Ben. Suddenly, the building cracked in two, the upper section teetering forward as if in slow motion. A wave of panicked screams distorted over the speakers. Mid-descent, the footage blurred out of focus as the camera's owner turned and fled for his life.

Adam switched off, afraid of what he might see. Starting to shake, he huddled back down under the covers. *Just like the White House. It's stood for so long, with history in every stone. And now—it's just gone.*

Nothing lasts forever, Adam thought gloomily. *Even when you're brought up to believe it will.*

He wished he could see Keera now, get the fear, the ordeal that lay ahead, all over and done with.

"I'd give anything to feel safe again," Adam murmured.

9 LATE NIGHT REUNION

Adam and Zoe stayed silent on the way to Fort Meade, lost in their thoughts. They were being driven together in an armored car in the middle of a convoy of military vehicles. The noise of the engine was mind-numbing, the ride enough to turn bones to jelly. They each cradled a gas mask on their lap—"to be deployed in case of an incident."

Images of Westminster in flames still haunted Adam's mind. The death count had risen to over seventy. He wondered what fresh horrors would follow.

It was after eleven when the armored car reached the base, and yet the grounds were still a floodlit hive of activity. Helicopters with searchlights swept the surrounding treetops on patrol. Rocket launchers and field guns were being positioned on the lawns, their operators hidden behind gas masks. Tanks guarded the driveways.

Zoe looked out through the thick, scuffed window. "Looks like they're ready for visitors."

"Will they ever be ready enough?" Adam muttered.

The armored car pulled up outside the on-site apartments. Barbed-wire fencing stretched all the way around the property now, and a well-manned checkpoint marked the entrance. Rocket launchers had been sited outside the building, pointing up at the night. The lights of a jet plane traced a circle high above.

"Adam!" came a familiar yell from the apartment block. "Adam, are you all right?"

"Dad!" A soldier pulled hard on the heavy-duty door, and Adam ran into his father's waiting arms. As Mr. Adlar started fussing gently over his bandaged hand, for a few moments the world felt better.

"Zoe? Sweetheart!" Eve Halsall pushed past them to where her daughter was being helped into her wheelchair by two soldiers, and flung her arms around her. "Thank God you two are all right."

"Yes, indeed." Dr. Marrs, wrapped up as ever in overcoat, hat and scarf, came shuffling out onto the porch. "It sounds as though the pair of you had a very close call."

"Dr. Marrs!" Adam was surprised. "What are you doing here?"

"In the wake of that meeting you attended, I've been appointed special adviser on the Geneflow threat for the

United Nations." Marrs patted him on the back and smiled. "I've been catching up with your parents to see what progress they've made with our scaly houseguest."

"And then we saw what had happened in London," said Mr. Adlar. "The carnage . . ."

"I couldn't believe it," said Zoe, steering her chair to join them. "So many people killed."

"A deplorable act," Marrs declared. "Let us hope the work with Keera will lead us closer to its perpetrators. In the meantime . . ." With a sad smile, he shook Zoe warmly by the hand. "Delighted to see you again, my dear. So pleased that you and your mother are on board for this project."

Eve's arms were tightly folded across her stained lab coat. "If I'd had one inkling of the danger Zoe would find herself in today, I'd never have accepted."

"I appreciate today has not been easy," Marrs said gently. "But this whole base is operating on the highest security alert. And if you come inside, my dear, I've a further safeguard."

Adam stood aside while Zoe steered herself a little erratically after Marrs. Then he, his dad and Eve followed them into the main entrance hall. He saw lights on behind the front door of the apartment opposite, but Marrs had beckoned Zoe into the Adlars' rooms and was spraying her with a fine mist from an unmarked canister.

"What is this stuff?" Zoe spluttered.

"Antistink." Adam ran up gratefully to get a coating.

"Geneflow came up with the stuff themselves. It takes away your scent so Z. beasts can't hunt you."

Marrs nodded. "Given today's events, to wear a little would seem a sensible precaution."

"Where did you get it, though?" Adam closed his eyes as Marrs crossed to him and sprayed him too. "Raptor Island?"

"There were supplies kept at the Geneflow base there, yes." Marrs removed his hat and waved it at the cloud of aerosol, then pushed a hand through his short, silvery hair. "The military analyzed the formula and created batches of their own for use in covert operations. Seems it puts guard dogs off the scent as well as dinosaurs."

"What about electroshock weapons?" asked Adam. "They're the only guns I've seen that can slow down a dinosaur."

"Colonel Oldman has requisitioned experimental Tasers not yet off the secret list," Marrs informed him. "Everything that can be done is being done."

Eve harrumphed. "A little late in the day. If the soldiers at Patuxent had been properly armed, maybe Adam and Zoe wouldn't have needed hospital treatment today."

Marrs nodded. "To live in hindsight is to live in paradise."

Zoe looked about the spartan apartment, unimpressed. "Paradise is a long, long way from this place."

"Would you rate it better or worse than Keera's cage?" Adam joked. "How is Keera, anyway?"

"Difficult," Mr. Adlar said with feeling.

"I've never seen anything like her." Eve sat down wearily in an armchair. "Disgusting—"

"Mum," Zoe protested.

"I mean, what's been done to her. That circuitry inserted into her brain."

Adam's dad nodded. "It contains a kind of security system designed to govern her thoughts. It's not that Keera won't answer questions—she physically can't."

"The fit she had on the tower block could have been due to a malfunction in the software," Dr. Marrs speculated, sinking into an armchair. "Most likely caused by an injury in battle; *something* made her break off from the attack on the White House to grab you."

"Since the breakdown, we think Keera's been pretty much deaf, dumb and blind," Adam's dad went on. "Anyway—we've made some progress. Eve's brain-wave modifiers put Keera into a temporary coma, and once her mental activity was down to near zero, I was able to start disabling the first layers of the security system."

"You mean," said Zoe, "Geneflow hid Keera's real self behind a bunch of locked doors—but between you both, you've started *un*locking them?"

"Well put," said Eve.

"What about Geneflow's snooping raptor?" said Adam quietly. "There's been no sign of it?"

"No," Marrs confirmed. "Only some unconfirmed

reports of a much larger creature glimpsed in the skies around here."

"Hence the firepower outside," Mr. Adlar muttered, "courtesy of Colonel Oldman."

"It's possible the raptor was collected by another Z. beast and taken to report to its masters," Marrs said thoughtfully. "It may have had all kinds of surveillance technology inserted into its brain."

"So Geneflow must know we're holding Keera," said Eve, "and that we're trying to get through to her."

Adam felt sick. "Will they try and get her back?"

All eyes turned to Dr. Marrs.

The old man gave a reassuring smile. "They won't find that easy. Our defenses are ten times stronger around the hangar at Patuxent than they are here." He paused. "The fact that Geneflow sent this raptor to inspect and attack suggests that Keera *does* possess important information as to their plans—if only we can get to it."

"Well, we've left the computers number-crunching the most likely bandwidths and wavelengths for communication." Eve glanced up at Mr. Adlar, who nodded. "We should be able to start trying first thing tomorrow."

"But there are layers and layers of security in that poor creature's brain," Mr. Adlar told Marrs. "Our lash-up may not work. And if that's the case, I'm getting Adam on the next flight out of Washington, far away from this whole affair."

"Given recent developments," said Marrs, "I'd say that this 'affair' is not confined to the United States. It is one of global concern."

Eve looked at the old man. "Are you talking about Westminster being stamped into the ground—or something else?"

Marrs seemed to hesitate. Then he stood up and began pacing slowly about the room, hands clasped behind his back. "We've been assuming that Geneflow are still in charge of their own creations. That reasoning could be flawed."

"What do you mean?" asked Mr. Adlar.

"General Winters and Colonel Oldman don't believe that Geneflow has the resources to carry out attacks of the kind we're now witnessing, not without help." Marrs paused again. "They suspect the involvement of an enemy power—most likely the Russian Federation."

"But surely Geneflow as a group is beyond politics," Mr. Adlar argued. "Jeff Hayden and Sam Josephs thought and planned only on scientific lines."

"Both deceased, Bill," Marrs reminded him. "We don't know who's in charge now."

"I know Russia and the US used to be at each other's throats," said Eve, "but surely the Cold War ended long ago."

Zoe spoke up: "Didn't you read about the US launching their antiballistic missile program in Europe? Russia responded by strengthening their air and space defense system. All those arms treaties all gone to . . ." She realized everyone was looking at her and raised her eyebrows. "What? I may be on wheels, but I can still surf the news."

"You're quite right, my dear," said Marrs. "The bad blood endures. Of course, the Russian Federation can't act openly against the West—it would be MAD."

Adam didn't follow. "Mad how?"

"MAD as in mutual assured destruction," murmured Mr. Adlar. "A nuclear war between East and West would have no winner. Each side has the power to inflict lethal damage upon the other—even after absorbing a surprise first strike."

Marrs nodded. "But if Russia attacks with Geneflow's living weapons, weapons so different and so powerful that traditional defenses are useless—"

"They could weaken their enemies," said Eve fearfully, "and take control."

"Colonel Oldman showed me the footage from that simulation you played, Adam." Dr. Marrs nodded gravely. "It seems likely the simulation was designed for training Z. beasts in the aftermath of a nuclear holocaust. That would also explain why they have stolen seeds and livestock DNA from the world's genetic reserves—to give Geneflow control over food supplies in the aftermath."

"All right, Jeremy, that's enough." Mr. Adlar stood up. "You have no facts to back this up, and you're scaring the children."

On principle, Adam opened his mouth to deny he was

afraid. But the words wouldn't come. "Like we weren't scared already," he managed, and Zoe nodded.

"I'm sorry, Bill, everyone. You're quite right." Marrs solemnly bowed his head to his audience. "Forgive an old man with too much on his mind. This has been a difficult day for you all; I must let you get some well-deserved sleep." Abruptly he raised his hat and hurried to the door. "Transport will be sent to collect you at six o'clock tomorrow morning. Sleep well, all."

The door clicked shut behind him.

"Sleep well." Zoe's voice was heavy with sarcasm. "After that bombshell?"

"Don't mention bombs," said Adam.

Mr. Adlar rubbed his eyes. "I just can't believe Geneflow would ally itself with any government."

"Let's hope we can get the truth out of Keera tomorrow," said Eve.

"It *is* tomorrow." Zoe checked her watch and groaned. "It's one A.M."

Adam crossed to the window, looked out over the troops and the defenses lined up in the floodlit grounds. *We've* got *to get through to Keera,* he thought miserably. *Whatever Geneflow are planning, they have to be stopped. Or else . . .*

Apocalypse?

He shook his head, breathed out softly.

Z. apocalypse.

10 "WHO CONTROLS YOU?"

The buzz of helicopters haunted Adam's dreams. He got up at five thirty, his eyes feeling full of grit. His dad, Eve and Zoe were already at the dining table picking at toast. Tired smiles were turned his way, but it seemed no one felt much like talking, Adam included.

He sat in silence the whole way to Patuxent, toying with the gas mask in his lap, listening to his bones rattle in the armored drum of the military transport. Only once did Zoe speak, an exclamation at the sheer size of the army presence all around the wildlife refuge.

That should be comforting, Adam told himself.

Once their driver had negotiated the various security requirements, in triplicate by the sound of things, and once Zoe was eased into her chair, the group was shepherded quickly into the hangar complex by armed guards. As they approached the laboratory, Adam could hear voices.

". . . sightings of giant flying creatures over Beijing, sir. But no indication of an actual attack on Chinese soil as yet."

"Could be the Z. beasts were in transit, sir, on their way to their next target."

"Or on their way home to their masters." That was Oldman's voice, Adam was sure. "Did the Chinese military attempt to intercept?"

"Planes were scrambled, sir, but no contact was made."

"Uh-huh. That's the official story."

"No satellite evidence as yet, but—"

An aide opened the door, and Adam saw Oldman had been talking with two junior officers, while three men in suits were inspecting Eve's miniature mountain of equipment, tweaking connections and trailing wires.

"Ah." The colonel dismissed the men reporting to him and greeted his new arrivals, his smile looking a little more forced than usual. "Good morning, all. Are we set?"

Eve looked ready to do some serious damage to the men messing with her stuff. "Could you kindly get away from that? It's a very delicate setup."

"Some very important people are going to set a lot of store by what we learn here today," said Oldman evenly.

"They want to know the systems are entirely accurate and reliable. So my friends here are going to work with you today."

Mr. Adlar looked at Eve. "Nice to be trusted, isn't it?"

"C'mon," Oldman cajoled them. "Everyone wants this effort to succeed. We're all on the same side—"

"Well, then, don't pull too hard on that cable!" Eve bustled off to accost the men, Oldman and Mr. Adlar in tow, while the soldiers watched, trying not to smirk.

Zoe gave Adam a long-suffering look. "They're nothing to do with us."

"Right." Adam tried to smile, but he was dwelling on the words he'd overheard. "A sighting of Z. beasts over China but no big attack," he said quietly. "Thought Russia was the enemy."

"Not too much love lost between China and the US either," Zoe mused. "They've clashed over trade, currency, foreign policy—"

"You know too much," Adam complained.

"Probably," Zoe agreed wryly. "I'm beginning to think ignorance is bliss."

Suddenly one of the suited men approached Adam. "Are you the interrogator?"

"Let's call him the *voice,* Charlie," said Oldman, breezing over. "I'll be directing the show, telling Adam here what to say through an earpiece."

Charlie hurried over to Adam and fitted something like a hearing aid to his ear and a small wireless microphone to his T-shirt. "Hopefully the computer's calculated the wavelength that'll get us past the remaining barriers in Keera's head—she'll understand you and be able to respond."

"Right." If Charlie felt Adam's heart thumping against the back of his hand, he made no comment.

The man looked at Zoe for a moment and turned to Oldman, discomfited. "And is, um, this person the interpreter?"

"Yes, I am," said Zoe loudly.

"She is," said Oldman. "Dr. Halsall will fit her daughter with the necessary equipment—now that she's quite finished vetting my science majors, here . . . ?"

Still grumbling under her breath, Eve got busy with a well-rehearsed drill, efficiently adorning Zoe with bundles of cables and pressure pads all around her head and neck.

"Cell phones switched off or in call disabled, please, everybody," Mr. Adlar called. "We don't want random signals messing up our connection."

Those with phones duly obeyed, and as Adam set his own cell to airplane mode, Oldman steered him out of the lab and signaled to Mr. Adlar to join them in the corridor that led to the hangar itself, where Keera was waiting.

"The Z. dactyl will be less sedated than yesterday," said the colonel, "but she's still all but glued to the floor."

Mr. Adlar grunted. "Just swear to me Adam and Zoe will be safe."

"I've got four armed men inside the hangar. At the first sign of trouble from the Z. dactyl, they'll get Adam and Zoe out—while we release heavy tranq gas to knock her out fast." Oldman nodded. "In addition, all troops are carrying brand-new shock weapons strong enough to bring down a herd of elephants. You saw how much fire-power we've got ranged outside, all around. No chances taken."

"I should hope not," said Mr. Adlar.

"And how about you? Are you going to deliver?"

Mr. Adlar nodded cautiously. "If the computers have done their math right, we'll soon have a hotline to Keera's head."

A low hum from behind them signaled the arrival of Zoe in her wheelchair, bundled up now in a huge coat and with blankets on her lap, her face half hidden by wires.

Even as Oldman opened his mouth to speak, Zoe said, "I'm ready."

Oldman glanced at Eve, who had followed her daughter out of the lab. She nodded. "Let's do this."

Adam felt queasy as he and Zoe were gently ushered into the hangar. His dad's hand on his shoulder did little to ease the rising tension as he took the last steps past the lockers . . .

And there he was, facing the giant pterosaur again.

Adam felt his insides rock at the sheer size and scale of the Z. dactyl—then recoiled a few steps as her eyes snapped open.

"It's all right, Adam," Oldman murmured. "She can't hurt you."

She's the one who's hurt, thought Adam as, under the chains and steel netting holding her down, she shifted her head to watch him approach. He shivered inside his parka. The chill of the darkened hangar seemed reflected in Keera's eyes.

Zoe trundled along in her wheelchair, drawing level with Adam as he walked toward the huge bars that caged off the pterosaur. Keera didn't react as Eve carefully scooped up the cradle of wiring that ran from her head and plugged the cables into the connectors Zoe wore like jewelry.

Adam closed his eyes as Mr. Adlar positioned the Think-Send headset. "I'll tell you what to say through your earpiece," Oldman reminded him. "There are cameras all around, and we'll be monitoring everything from the control room."

"Got it," Adam breathed. He felt his dad's hands on his shoulders one more time, then heard the echo of retreating footsteps. Keera's eyes were still wide and staring.

Zoe looked at him. He tried to give her a smile, but his lips felt stiff, uncertain. Everyone was counting on them; whatever they found out here would reach the world's most important people before the day was out. *And we're just kids,* he thought, his confidence flailing. *We don't count, really, we—*

Oldman's voice crackled into his ear. "Testing, one, two. Adam, can you hear me?"

Not trusting his voice, Adam looked for the nearest security camera and nodded, holding up his thumb. A few seconds later, Zoe did the same thing.

"Okay, Adam," came his dad's calm voice, "I'm opening the signal channels, but we're still guessing on the precise wavelength. Try to make contact."

With a deep breath, Adam stared at Keera and forced himself to concentrate. He could already feel a kind of hardness to his thoughts, a familiar sensation of strength and control. Most times it meant he was opening the door to a virtual world, where he could run around adventuring as someone else. But right now the fiction was fact, and he was just a mental mouthpiece, projecting words into the messed-up mind of a gargantuan monster.

Do it, he told himself. *The sooner this is over—*

"It's not over!" shrieked Zoe, convulsing in her chair.

The sudden sound and movement was like a spike in Adam's chest. On instinct, he made toward her to see if she was okay, but babbling broke out in his ear. "Don't touch her!" Oldman snapped. "The responses from Keera just went through the roof."

"I'm okay," Zoe called shakily.

"I don't understand." Eve's voice was low through his earpiece; Adam could hear controls being worked, buttons pressed. "Contact never happened so fast before."

Mr. Adlar's voice broke in. "We didn't even ask anything. But with her mind damaged, perhaps it's just random—"

"No." Adam's voice sounded small and lost in the cavernous hangar. "I reckon she picked up on something I was thinking. I was wishing this was over—"

"It's not over," Zoe hissed, rocking in the chair. "She knows that, but . . . She's so strong, Mum. It's not just impressions and feelings. She thinks with *words* I can understand."

Eve's voice came, quiet and breathless. "This has never happened before."

"Oldman's right," Mr. Adlar muttered. "Since the Think-Send signal is built around Adam's brain waves, his thoughts are super-compatible with the system. Like an aerial booster brings in a sharper TV picture, he's amplifying the signal in and out of Keera's brain."

Adam had broken out in a cold sweat. "What do you want me to ask her?"

"It's not over," Zoe said again, in a spooky stage whisper. "Who . . . are you?" She spoke normally again. "Mum, she wants to know who we are."

"Say we're friends," Oldman instructed. "We want to help her."

"We're friends," Adam parroted. "We want—"

"The creator," Zoe hissed. "Creator . . . my friend—"

"No," Adam said automatically. "The people who created you are *not* your friends. We are."

"She's not getting it," Zoe reported. "Creator's her friend . . . She keeps thinking it."

Oldman spoke again in Adam's ear, quiet and urgent. "Adam, we need to know about the creator, okay? Who created her?"

"She wants to know why can't she move," Zoe said, words jerking from her mouth. "Heavy is wrong for her . . . She hates this place. She wants the sky back. Creator gives her flight—"

"Adam, come on," Oldman urged him.

Looking into the pterosaur's dark eyes, Adam pictured the words as he heard them. "Who . . . is . . . controlling . . . you?"

"No one," snarled Zoe. "No one will ever control her. Not again. Not anyone. No . . . not ever. The creator . . ." Zoe's voice was becoming more strangled. "Where's the sun? Hates this place. Why have you made dark?"

"Keep with it, Adam," Oldman insisted. "Her creators, who are they and what do they want?"

"GO!" screamed Zoe as a spasm wrenched through Keera's huge, scaly form. Desperately, the Z. dactyl squirmed on the filthy floor, as if trying to reach the thick bars. Her metal bonds scraped and clattered as she shook her head from side to side, wings and tail twitching.

Behind him, Adam heard the cocking of weapons as the soldiers reacted.

"Men, hold your fire," Oldman ordered.

Don't, Keera, thought Adam desperately. *You'll hurt yourself. It's all right—we only want to talk.*

"Can't talk," Zoe said, her voice rising. "She says . . . she *mustn't* talk. There's something in the way." The pterosaur's huge, hooked jaws pressed up against a gap in the bars and her eyes narrowed with pain.

"High adrenal activity." Eve sounded worried. "Vital signs through the roof."

"We should call a stop," said Mr. Adlar.

"Keera needs the sky!" Zoe bellowed.

"No!" Oldman snapped. "Tell her, Adam, she can have the sky back if she talks. Who made her?"

Adam felt sick, tried to concentrate. "Who . . . made you?"

"Adam!" Zoe screamed suddenly, jerking in her chair. "Adam, help me."

The soldiers in the hangar looked at each other as Adam ran to her side. "What is it?" She reached up for his shoulder, and he offered support as she pulled herself into a standing position, the blankets falling from her lap.

"Wait," said Oldman, "what do you think you're doing?"

Zoe looked up at the nearest security camera. "We can't just throw words at her and expect her to toss them back," she called, the echoes ringing around the vaulted space. "The computers in her head are twisting her thoughts. It hurts. She's an animal—this isn't her voice."

"We need to continue," Oldman insisted.

"Not like this." Zoe broke away from Adam's hold and hopped toward Keera.

"Zoe, no!" Eve's voice burst from the receiver.

"Men, stand by to restrain the girl," said Oldman. The soldiers instantly stiffened, alert.

Zoe reached out for one of the thick metal bars to lean against, then sank to the ground in front of Keera's colossal head. She hesitated—then reached out a hand through the metal webbing that held Keera pinned to the floor and placed her fingers against the creature's jaw.

Adam winced at the protests of Eve and his father in his ear. On instinct, he lunged forward to grab Zoe's arm, to pull her away.

"No." She caught hold of his wrist and looked at him through the tangle of wires hanging down from her forehead. "Adam, you don't know what it's like to be treated like a thing. A thing that doesn't feel, that *isn't* right, that has no voice of its own. Well, I do. And this creature's so scared, so confused. We need to help her find her *own* voice."

"Come on, kid," said one of the soldiers. "Get away from that thing—"

"No!" Zoe said fiercely. "I know how to do this, and I'm not stopping."

"We'll see about that," growled Oldman.

"Get heavy with her, and she'll never help you," Eve warned. "Hold off with the guards. Let me talk to her."

Zoe had turned back to Keera, whose big eyes were still closed. "It's okay," she murmured. "It's okay."

"All right," Oldman said. "Get in there. Make it quick."

Keera, thought Adam, closing his eyes, *we really need to know about the people who sent you out to hurt and kill. We need to find them so we can stop them. That's what we want to do.*

The beast's eyes snapped open suddenly.

Zoe flinched, but kept her hand in place against its skin. "I'm seeing someplace . . . There's, like, static in the way, like snow . . ."

"Eve, wait!" That was Adam's dad, back in his ear. "Look here. We're getting something visual."

I want to stop the people who did this to you, Keera. The fervent words came tumbling through Adam's mind. *I want this nightmare to be over.* "Please, Keera," he said out loud, "if you can tell us anything that will lead us to the people who made you this way—"

"Yes," Zoe whispered. "Free . . . lead . . . I will lead . . . free . . ."

Then she screamed and fell, knocked backward as Keera's body spasmed with seismic force. The beast's jaws were bubbling a bloody spit. The soldiers advanced warily from the shadows, guns raised.

"Get the kids out of there!" Mr. Adlar shouted.

"Hold on to that," said Oldman. "If it's another fit, it'll pass—"

"Readings are different this time," Eve broke in. "She's excited about something."

Terrified, Adam hauled Zoe away, the wires and connections unplugging as he did so.

"We've lost contact," Eve reported. "Zoe?"

"She's all right," Adam said quickly. The whole hangar shook as Keera rocked and flapped her scaly bulk, impotent against her chains, pounding echoes doubling and redoubling through the cold gloom. "Zoe, you're not connected to Keera now. Are you all right?"

Zoe's eyes were blank, but her lips moved. Adam couldn't hear the words for the thrashing and booming. He put his ear to her mouth and caught the whispers. "Give me sky back . . . You'll be sorry . . . Hunters . . ."

"Zoe?" Adam was becoming more frightened now. It was like she was in a trance. "Zoe, snap out of it."

She shook her head. "Hunters hunting . . . sky . . . quickly—"

"That thing's getting loose!" yelled one of the soldiers as a huge black split tore through the concrete floor. He raised his stubby shock weapon and fired bolts of brilliant yellow light into the cage, but Keera went on thrashing against her chains.

"Evacuate!" The colonel's command bit into Adam's brain just as Keera finally wrenched the gigantic sprawl of one wing clear of the ground. "Hit the tranq gas . . ."

Adam scrabbled for his respirator. "Hunters here!" Zoe screamed.

A soldier grabbed her under the arms and started hauling her away. But then the floor shook so hard it threw them all flat on their backs. Adam's earpiece was jarred loose, and he dropped the gas mask as a massive spray of concrete debris erupted from the ground, turning the air to choking powder. Zoe's would-be rescuer let her drop as a chunk of rock smashed into the back of his head and he collapsed.

"Help!" Adam shouted, staring around wildly. It felt like the whole place was crashing down around them. *How can Keera be strong enough to do all this?*

A searing blaze of yellow light jerked his attention to the other three soldiers, all firing their shock weapons—not at Keera, but in the opposite direction. *What are they . . . ?*

A giant, reptilian head came swooping out of the hangar's shadows. Huge jaws festooned with teeth clamped down on three of the still-firing soldiers, lifting them into the smoky air with a careless swing of the muscular neck.

"Here!" Zoe shrieked again as the shifting shadows solidified into three identical, hulking dinosaur creatures. A fourth was climbing out from a gigantic hole in the floor. They looked like Godzilla's grown-up cousins—like Zed, only darker, larger, even meatier.

They must've come for Keera. Adam held stock-still,

petrified. *The raptor told them where she was, and when they saw the outside of the hangar was too well defended, they tunneled underneath to reach her.*

Scaly hides glistening in the half-light, the giant monsters stamped toward him.

11 A SINKING FEELING

Adam didn't know what was riskier—running or staying put and hoping he'd be overlooked. These monsters were clearly the hunters that Keera—and Zoe—had mentioned, come to save their own kind from enemy hands.

But then, why did she try to warn us they were coming?

One of the Z. rexes smashed a thick, sinewy tail against the floor, and a fresh cloud of dust billowed out. Adam pulled on his fallen respirator. What had happened to the tranquilizer gas that was supposed to flood out if Keera got too agitated? Perhaps the raptor scout had warned its masters and the scaly giants had ruptured the gas pipes as they tunneled their way through.

The dust lingered in the air, a ragged smoke screen

to hide Adam as he scurried over to Zoe, lying semi-conscious on the floor. *We're cloaked in antistink,* he thought. *They can't sniff us out, so if we can just stay out of sight and wait for Dad and the army to get us . . .*

He held his breath as three of the creatures lurched past him, their movements synchronized, making for Keera's pen. The fourth Z. rex smashed through the line of lockers—to expose a squad of troops massing to attack it. As the monster roared defiance, the soldiers fired their shock weapons, shrouding it in a sickly yellow haze. Undeterred, it stomped and kicked and tore into the irritants around it.

Oldman's new guns aren't enough. Crouched beside Zoe, Adam felt sick with terror. *There's no way out.*

He watched as the three nearest Z. rexes gripped the bars of Keera's cage with enormous clawed hands and bent them apart. Keera writhed on the ground before them, straining her mutilated wings to be free.

"Don't!" cried Zoe suddenly, and Adam shushed her frantically. "Don't let them take me!"

"Keep quiet," hissed Adam, "or they will for sure."

But Zoe wouldn't be calmed. "Want the sky," she shouted. "Adam! Free in the sky!"

Adam clamped a hand over her mouth. Zoe was raving, rolling her eyes, getting louder. "Shhh." Panic-stricken, Adam looked over to where the creatures were tearing the wire netting from Keera's wings, smashing the equipment ranged around her.

Then one of the giant monsters stamped down on the pterosaur's head.

Adam gasped, but Zoe shrieked as though she'd felt the blow herself. *She must still be linked to Keera,* Adam realized, his guts cartwheeling. *That mad stuff she was spouting . . . were they Keera's words?* Another of the monsters smashed its tail down on Keera's back, and Zoe cried out again. Her back arched—then she fell limp and silent.

"Zoe!" Adam could see she was still breathing, apparently asleep. He looked over to the exit—the surviving soldiers were in retreat, and the Z. rex was smashing its way out into the corridor in pursuit. The other three Godzillas were still bearing down on Keera, kicking and stamping and slicing at her bloodied body. Somehow she managed to wrench herself clear of her attackers and launch awkwardly into the air. But huge claws lunged for her, one catching her by the tail.

Adam could hardly bring himself to watch as Keera twisted in midair and rammed the point of her jaws into her attacker's eye. A howl of pain filled the hangar space as the claws unclenched and Keera pulled free, turning tightly with powerful sweeps of her wings. But while one of the Z. rexes was distracted, swiping blood and juice from its ruined eye, the other two were still murderously active. One stretched its neck to bite into Keera's body, but she turned again—and rammed her beak into the toothy cavern of its mouth, forcing her jaws down its throat while slashing at its neck with her sicklelike talons. The dinosaur toppled backward, smashing into the bars and trampling its one-eyed partner as Keera yanked her head away, sending thick strings of blood splattering in a wide arc. Her victim fell and slammed into one of the loosened bars, which broke away from the ceiling and fell with a mind-jarring clang, quickly followed by a large chunk of the roof.

"Zoe, come on, wake up," Adam begged her. "We've *got* to get out of here!"

He watched as Keera flew up and scraped her vast beak against the girders in the roof, clawing at the steel bands that held her jaws shut. But the third Z. rex was ready to avenge its fallen friends. Its back broke open with a wet, crunching sound, and two stubby wings unfolded. Like some prehistoric dragon, it propelled itself upward in short, speedy bursts—as the metal restraints finally fell from Keera's beak and struck the ground only yards from where Adam stood.

Snarling and shrieking, the two flying monsters locked together in deadly combat.

Got to take a chance—or die. With fierce determination, Adam managed to lift Zoe over his shoulder, ready to make a dash for the exit. Straining under her weight, Adam staggered across the hangar. Halfway to the doors, he chanced a look behind. Keera was trying to tear herself away from her attacker, biting at its wings.

Then he realized with a lurch that the one-eyed Z. rex

had seen them. It rose up, brows locked together in a hateful glare, teeth as big as stalactites gleaming. With a blood-blistering roar, it snaked out its neck, jaws opening wide to devour them. Adam didn't even have time to scream—

—before a rush of air almost knocked him off his feet, and he and Zoe were snatched away by Keera's butcher's-hook claws. He gasped with pain as the pterosaur's grip crushed Zoe hard against him, choked on dust in the dizzying rush of flight. He saw the hole in the roof zoom closer—and then in a gale of noise and debris, Keera tore straight through into her treasured sky.

Dangling with Zoe, helpless in Keera's claws, Adam let loose a howl of terror as the pterosaur banked to the right. The fourth of the monsters had smashed its way outside and was taking on a big-time military retaliation. Its skin was scorched and blackened, and blood ran from huge wounds in its side—but from the scattered corpses and tanks stamped into the ground, Adam could tell the Z. rex was giving as good as it got. *Dad, where are you?* Adam saw no sign of him, or Eve or Colonel Oldman. But the laboratory looked to be on fire.

"Dad!" he bellowed.

And somehow, the embattled Z. rex seemed to hear. It twisted its long neck to look straight up at him. Instantly it flicked out its gruesome, sticky wings and threw itself through the air toward them. As Keera sped away over the grounds of the wildlife refuge, Adam swore when the other three monsters, two of them wounded, rose up from the shattered hangar, their eerie stealth shields shimmering.

Keera descended sharply. Adam was almost sick, clutching Zoe, his stomach jammed in his throat. *She's going to crash and kill us—*

But at the last moment, she leveled out barely a yard from the long grass and let Adam and Zoe drop. They both fell like deadweights and Adam gasped, winded, as Zoe landed on top of him. He saw Keera fly on. *She's leaving us.* Hope torched in his chest for a moment. *She knows that those things are after her, not us, so she's . . .*

She's coming back.

Adam struggled up with Zoe in his arms. Keera circled and landed beside them, with incredible lightness for a beast so big. Her mauled jaws cranked open, her eyes wide and bright. She shifted her weight from foot to foot, impatient or uneasy, and made deep chittering sounds in the back of her throat, her gaze meeting his. Adam had the unmistakable feeling she was trying to communicate something.

Adam looked behind him. A blood-soaked shine low over the landscape told that the four Godzillas were coming for them. *And there's nowhere we can go, there's . . .*

Keera opened her jaws still wider, her wings at full-stretch, corded muscles there twitching. Was she trying to show him something? Adam remembered Zed had stored stuff for a mission like explosives in a fleshy compartment inside his mouth; did Keera have something similar? With Zoe still in his arms, he took a step closer . . .

And Keera curled one wing around them both, sweeping them into her giant jaws. "No!" Adam shouted as he stumbled into the dark, slippery space. *She's gonna eat us, gonna swallow us.* He landed on top of Zoe in a sticky hollow beneath Keera's rasping tongue. It felt like wet rubber and smelled like . . .

Adam was almost sick with the stench of putrefying flesh. Keera's mouth was a narrow, glistening cave, its undulating walls dripping with globs of blood and saliva. Gooey strands of half-chewed meat clogged the gaps between her reddened teeth. Adam covered his mouth with his hand, tried to get back out.

But then the huge jaws slammed shut and Keera's scythelike teeth knitted tightly together, plunging the damp cave into darkness. An eerie rushing, pounding sound filled the darkness; Adam realized it must be the pterosaur's heartbeat.

"Zoe?" He reached out and his hand brushed against her arm. Then he heard the muffled beating of vast wings and felt a sickening lurch as Keera took to the air. *Oh, my God, we're gonna die . . .*

The massive, fleshy slab of Keera's tongue flopped down on top of him and Zoe, wedging them inside the cavity. He was both repulsed and relieved—at least it might keep them from disappearing down her throat and ending up as another meal. But the stink of it . . . He clung to Zoe, not knowing if he wanted her to wake up or stay blissfully oblivious to what was happening.

Keera's body spasmed wildly, a rumble building somewhere in her guts. Her tongue flicked upward as she opened her jaws wide to release a terrifying roar of anger.

She's getting her voice back. Jamming his hands over his ears, Adam let Zoe go and peered over the side of the compartment. A rush of air billowed into the cavity, like they were in a roller coaster bursting from out of a tunnel—and a bloodied, battered Z. rex filled Adam's vision. He yelled as he saw it swooping down toward them at incredible speed, claws outstretched, mouth open, its yellow eyes burning with fury. At the last moment, Keera rolled sharply to the left to avoid the attack, and Adam was flung backward into the cavity.

Rubbing his bruised back, Adam crouched low next to Zoe, hanging on to her again as Keera's tongue flapped down and scraped over them once more. It felt disgusting, rasping and rubbery, soaking his skin with a sharp, stinking fluid. He sensed a rapid succession of body blows jolting the creature from side to side. *Those things are never going to give up,* he thought desperately. *They're going to knock her out of the sky.*

But it seemed Keera wasn't about to give up either. She swooped and dived, answering each vicious assault with a choking screech of defiance.

Adam's stomach lurched. *It's like we're living a video game, and God knows who has got the controls.* Every few seconds, he was afforded a fleeting view of Keera's attackers through her half-opened mouth. From what he could make out, at least three of the Z. rexes were circling her in some kind of formation, taking it in turns to attack.

Another jolt, harder this time. Adam's internal organs swapped places as Keera suddenly plummeted downward. Dizziness overwhelmed him. *Going to crash* . . . He hung on to Zoe, crushed up against her in the darkness. *We hardly even know each other, and now* . . . Keera's tongue flapped wildly overhead. Adam gasped as an ice-cold gale from outside whipped about his face before the great mouth slammed shut once more and he waited for the inevitable collision . . .

But it didn't come. At least, not in the way he expected. Keera hit something—but the impact was almost cushioned. Adam sensed Keera's body rolling gently from side to side. The steady pumping of her heartbeat signaled she was still alive and in one piece.

As the seconds passed, Adam allowed himself to believe the attack was over. But how? Why had the creatures given up like that? His ears popped, as if the pressure was changing around him, and he swallowed hard to clear them. What next? With a sinking feeling, Adam realized he was entirely out of options, literally along for the ride. The dark, cramped space was making him feel claustrophobic, the stench was making him feel sick.

What is that goo plastered all over her tongue? he wondered. *Please, don't let it be something that makes us easier to digest.*

Then Adam felt a sharp elbow jab him in his chest. Zoe was stirring at last.

"What the . . . ?" Zoe's voice rose as she started to come round. "Adam, is that you? Where are we?" She went rigid. "Ugh, that stink!"

Adam held her by the shoulders and shushed her, trying to calm her down. "It's all right, we're . . . we're inside Keera."

"She's *eaten* us?"

"No!" Adam said quickly. "In her jaws. I think she's taking us away someplace."

"But what *happened*?" Zoe sounded distraught. "It's all so hazy. I was seeing something in Keera's mind . . . a place with snow . . . and then it was like I was actually inside there."

"The place with snow?"

"No." Zoe sounded husky, hesitant. "I mean . . . inside Keera's mind. It's like . . . we touched."

"Well, now you've been eaten." Adam frowned. "Do you remember the Z. rexes, those dinosaur monsters that attacked us?"

"Kind of . . ."

"I don't understand why they tried to kill her." He paused, feeling dizzy and disoriented in the absolute dark. "I mean, if they wanted to stop her talking to us, why not just set her free so she could escape with them?"

"Because Keera's not on their side anymore." Zoe sounded fervent. "I'm *sure* she's not. She . . . she doesn't want to be owned by anyone."

"So why did she shove us in her mouth and fly off with us?"

"To save us," said Zoe, "why else?"

"I can think of one reason." Adam sighed. "Keera snatched me out of nowhere back in DC, then had her fit. Maybe her programming is making her pick up where she left off. This compartment under her tongue could've been made for carrying people—"

"Shhh. Wait."

Adam heard her shiver in the clammy darkness. "What?"

"It's getting colder. And listen."

Adam heard a quiet gurgling noise. Keera's guts or . . . ? *No. Oh, no way.*

"Adam," Zoe breathed, "I think we're underwater. *That's* how she got away from those things."

In the dark, disturbing near-silence, Adam remembered Dr. Marrs's words back at the Pentagon: "Z. rexes can fly huge distances—so why bother to create Z. dactyls?"

Perhaps because Z. dactyls aren't just creatures of the air—they can swim too.

"This is crazy." Zoe grabbed Adam's arm, making him

jump. "Totally crazy. I mean, she's a flying reptile, not a swimming one! How can she do this?"

"Because Geneflow must have had some reason to make her that way. What I don't get is, why aren't we drowning right now?"

"Keera's jaws must be airtight. Which means . . ." Zoe groaned quietly. "Which means the oxygen in here will be running out."

"We'll suffocate." Fear prickled through his body. "Hey!" he shouted. "Keera, we need air in here! Surface! Come on!"

"Stop it," Zoe urged him. "You'll only use up the air faster."

"Well, you try! You're the one who's meant to be so close to her . . ." He trailed off, his anger blowing out as quickly as it had ignited. "I'm sorry, Zoe."

"Like it matters." She found his fingers and squeezed them. "I'm sorry too. I really felt that Keera wouldn't hurt us. Guess I was wrong."

"She's an animal. Why should it occur to her that we need air?" Adam shrugged helplessly in the blackness. "Anyway. I guess she's got to come up sometime to breathe again."

"But if she doesn't anytime soon . . ."

Zoe left the thought hanging. *Saving her breath,* Adam supposed. Already he was feeling kind of woozy—imagination, or the first fingers of suffocation at his throat? If Keera didn't surface, then it would all be over for them just as surely as if one of the Z. rexes had caught them. The pointlessness of it all crashed down on Adam, and his mood became as black as the prison of flesh all around. He felt strangely tired. He wasn't sure if it was the shifting movement of Keera's body beneath him, but there was a spinning sensation building inside his head; he was starting to lose all sensation in his body.

He searched out Zoe's fingers, tried to focus on the feeling. But it was no use. Adam slumped back, his last thoughts melting away as consciousness fled and left him to the darkness.

12 NUMBER NOT AVAILABLE

Adam awoke with an aching stomach.

He blinked. His mouth was dry, and he felt starved. His body was warm, but the air was icy on his face.

Memories flooded back.

He realized that he was staring not at Keera's blood-stained mouth, but instead at a high corrugated metal ceiling. The sun's feeble rays shone through a cracked skylight. *I'm alive!*

Sitting bolt upright, Adam found he'd been half buried beneath sleeping bags still in their torn plastic packaging. Zoe was curled up next to him, asleep and similarly swamped with sleeping bags. A shedload of groceries—from cans and packets to fresh and frozen meat—lay littered around them in the middle of a huge, derelict warehouse.

It's like a nest, thought Adam. He grabbed a dented can of peaches and yanked hard on the ring pull; his bandaged hand felt much better.

As he slurped down the juice and slithery segments inside, he looked about him more closely. The writing on the labels was in a funny language he didn't recognize. Behind him were two enormous wooden doors, one of which was hanging off its hinges. It looked as if Keera had made a dramatic entrance.

Where is she?

A movement in the corner of his eye made Adam turn to the other end of the cavernous warehouse. Crouched in one corner, half hidden in shadow, was Keera. The wounds around her head and jaws seemed almost healed, and she was feeding on the remains of an animal, ravenously ripping the creature's flesh from its bones. *You didn't pick* that *thing up at the local store,* thought Adam; he glimpsed ragged patches of white fur spattered with blood and a grisly pile of discarded skin and bones.

Adam swallowed hard. Judging by the size of her victim, it looked like Keera was devouring a polar bear. Had she raided a zoo as well as the local 7-Eleven? Where *were* they? He fumbled for another can, apricot halves this time, and quickly downed them, almost choking in his haste. He wiped his sticky mouth, mind racing. If he ran now, could he escape to fetch help—or would the Z. dactyl come after him?

He was distracted by a whimper. Zoe was stirring in her sleep, her only leg lashing out at some invisible attacker. *She's having nightmares.* Uncertainly, Adam leaned over and shook her. Zoe's eyes suddenly snapped open, her features twisting in fear as she gasped for breath.

"Zoe, it's okay. We're safe." He pushed aside some bottles of cooking oil to get at a carton of drink and passed it to her. "I don't know how, but we made it."

While Zoe tore the cardboard open and drank deeply, Adam found some more peaches and opened them up. Zoe dropped the carton and snatched the can from his hands, scooping the fruit into her mouth. "Where are we?" she mumbled through a sticky mouthful. "Why's it so cold?"

"Ask the polar bear." Adam nodded to Keera's bloodthirsty feast in the shadows. "I guess Keera must've surfaced for air after all. I blacked out, I don't know how long for . . ." He frowned, started patting his pockets. "But if I can find my phone, that'll tell us, right?"

Zoe finished the peaches, wiped her hands on a sleeping bag and pulled her own phone from her jeans pocket. "Mine's out of battery. Weird, I thought I had plenty of charge."

Scanning the screen, Adam saw his own battery was almost flat—then did a double take as he saw the date on the scuffed screen. "No way. That's got to be wrong, it's . . ." He showed Zoe the screen. "It's two days since we were in the hangar."

"Two *days*?"

"Seven o'clock in the morning, almost forty-eight hours." He sniffed himself and grimaced. "Guess that explains one or two things." He tugged at the bandages on his hand and saw that the cut was now healing well.

Zoe looked at him wildly. "Mum will be freaking. She hates to let me out of her sight. Has your dad called?"

"My phone's been in flight mode since we went into the hangar—you can't make or take calls." He disabled the setting and waited, praying he would get a signal.

"How were we out for all that time?" Zoe was opening a can of corned beef with the little metal key. "Last I remember, we were running out of air. I got so dizzy . . ."

"And sleepy," Adam agreed thoughtfully. "How could we sleep for two days, unless—" He remembered the chemical stink on Keera's tongue. "Unless we were helped. Maybe there was something in her saliva that *made* us sleep."

"Like an anesthetic, you mean?" Zoe finished opening the can and bit a big chunk from the pressed meat inside. "Why would there be?"

"Dr. Marrs told me and Dad how a load of scientific genius types had been kidnapped by Geneflow, with creatures heard overhead around the same time." Adam took his own mouthful of the salty, freezing meat, thinking hard. "And Keera opened her jaws for us to get inside like it was the most natural thing in the world."

Zoe's eyes widened. "You think Z. dactyls did the kidnapping?"

"Well, they're designed for it. Just tuck the victim under your tongue, out of the way, stop them struggling with some drugged spit, then slip into stealth mode—or vanish into water. Gone without a trace." Adam ate some more and kept staring at the phone, willing a signal to appear in the top left corner. "When Keera took me the first time, she only grabbed me round the ribs, so I didn't get sleepy . . ."

"She wasn't trying to kidnap you." Zoe swigged some more from the carton. "In the hangar when she was talking about her creator, I'm pretty sure she didn't mean anyone at Geneflow. She was talking about *you*."

Adam finally looked up from his phone. "Me?"

"That part of her that doesn't want anyone telling her what to do, that wants to be free—she associates it with you. Or whatever bit of you got left behind in those Think-Send brain waves." Zoe ripped open a half-crushed box of biscuits. "I think a part of you's been haunting her head from the day she was born. Maybe she sensed you were near, back in DC, and just *had* to find you."

"Maybe." Adam felt seriously weirded out, but had to admit it was the likeliest explanation. In the past, traces of his personality had bled through Zed's programming, with the creature tearing apart New Mexico to find him.

And even Loner, the raptor with a human mind, had felt linked to Adam, thanks to Think-Send. He glanced over at Keera, remembering the pain in her eyes on the rooftop, the way she'd looked at him as if desperate for help.

And I was too busy being scared to death to think of giving it.

"She may think she knows me, but you're the one who seems to know her." Adam went back to staring at his phone. "You said you'd touched her mind—and even when you were unhooked from the cables, you were shouting about wanting the sky, and the hunters and stuff."

"Keera's thoughts." Zoe nodded, speaking through a mouthful of biscuit crumbs. "So freaky. It was like she was broadcasting her feelings, and I was a radio picking them up."

Adam looked at her warily. *How could that happen?* But it wasn't as if the rest of the world made a bunch of sense right now. "Can you tune in and find out what happens next? Why Keera's brought us here—wherever here is?" He broke off as a weak signal crept into his phone beside the word *Telenor.* "Finally. I'll call Dad. He must be going crazy." He dialed the number, but it wouldn't connect; he got an automated voice saying something in a foreign language. He tried again, with the same result.

"What's up?" asked Zoe.

Adam put the recorded voice on speakerphone. "I can't get through. My phone doesn't allow international calls, and we were rushed off to the States so quickly I didn't even think about asking Dad to change it." He put down the can of corned beef, feeling sick. "Zoe, we're not in America anymore." He switched back to the main screen and selected the satellite map. "Let's see if this tells us anything."

Zoe wriggled over beside him. They both stared at the screen like they meant to burn holes in it, until finally a blue circle appeared on the grid. Adam swept his fingers across the touch screen to zoom out and the map began to load a moth-eaten coastline in pixellated pieces.

"This is crazy," Zoe whispered. "Looks to me like . . . Scandinavia."

Adam looked at her. "Telenor. *Nor* as in Norway? That's got to be thousands of miles from Maryland."

"And Keera made it in just two days?"

The blue circle on the screen went on pulsing serenely. "Perhaps that's another reason why Geneflow bred pterosaurs alongside Z. rexes," Adam supposed. "They not only swim for whatever reason, they're faster in the air."

Zoe jumped as another huge bone was discarded on the pile. "Maybe Keera's stopped here to fuel up and rest."

"But where's our destination?" Adam surveyed the sleeping bags and the edible litter all around. "She's stocked up for us. I guess she sensed we'd need food and drink after two days."

A chime from the phone made them both jump. A text message had come through: *Voice Mail: Caller Unknown.*

"At least I can still receive calls." Adam stabbed at the soft buttons on the phone. "But can I pick up messages . . . ?"

As if in answer, the calm tones of his voice mail sounded over the speaker: "Thursday," it said sunnily. "Three fifty-four A.M."

"That's yesterday," Zoe realized.

Then a familiar voice whispered urgently out from the phone. "Adam? It's me, Dad."

"Dad!" Adam held the phone closer, straining to catch every hoarse word.

"I pray you're all right, that Keera saved you and Zoe, that you get this. Ad, they've taken me—Geneflow. The raid on the hangar, those monsters took me and Eve . . ."

Zoe gripped Adam's arm. "What?"

"Shhh!" Adam hissed, straining to hear.

"We were set up, Ad. Colonel Oldman and Dr. Marrs—they've been working for Geneflow all along. Whatever happens—don't tell Oldman *or* Marrs where you are."

No. Adam shook his head, throat burning with the threat of tears. *No, they can't have been.*

"I know you've been tricked in the past by messages you thought were from me, but this is for real. Remember your birthday meal at Brown's, when Stevie got that candle stuck up his nose? Remember those beige pants you got me Christmas before last, three sizes too big? It's me, Ad. Eve and I, we've been taken to Geneflow's headquarters—where Keera was reared. We think it's some way inland from the port of Murmansk in Russia. We're all right for now; Geneflow needs us to work for them. But . . ." There was a long pause, then his voice dropped lower. "I have to go. Please—try to find someone you can trust. Oldman and Marrs will be out to get Keera—and you and Zoe too. Don't believe anything they say. Be brave, Ad."

The phone went silent.

"To delete the message, press two," came the automated voice. "To play the message again, press three."

Adam pressed three and listened again, tears squeezing through his eyelids, Zoe still clutching his arm. "This can't be happening," he muttered, shivering now in the warehouse chill. "Losing Dad . . . tricked by people we thought were friends . . . it can't be happening again."

The message ended just the same: "Be brave, Ad."

"Brave. Right." Adam put down the phone and looked at Zoe. "So . . . what the hell do we do now?"

"Lose it completely?" Zoe looked crushed. "I mean, you're positive that was your dad, right?"

"I know his voice. And all that stuff he said . . ." Adam sighed, remembering that carefree night at Brown's last year. It felt like another life. "Only he'd know that."

"Then if Dr. Marrs is a part of this, and also Oldman, what *can* we do?" Zoe was working herself up into a state. "Oh, Mum . . . if anything happens to her, what am I—"

"Don't think that way," Adam urged her. "Maybe Keera can find them. She was reared there. She must know where the place is."

"That's it!" Zoe grabbed the phone from him, started pressing buttons. "The map, look. Norway's well on the way to Russia. Adam, I think Keera's been taking us to this Geneflow base all along!"

"I don't see—"

"What was the last thing you asked us—asked *Keera* in the hangar? For anything that might lead to the ones who did this to her, remember?"

Adam blinked and wiped his nose. "I *did* ask that, yeah. And you were muttering on, something about being free, and—"

"I will *lead*! That's what I said. Lead you to the ones who did it." Zoe looked over at Keera in wonder. "She wants to be free, Adam, and you promised if she led us to Geneflow, she *would* be free. That's why we're here. I know it. This is just a pit stop on the way to that base!"

A low chittering came from the corner, like confirmation. Keera had finished her meal and was watching them with those cold, black eyes.

Adam couldn't meet that stare. "She was supposed to tell us stuff that could lead the army to Geneflow," he muttered. "Not take the two of us. What are we supposed to do by ourselves? A couple of kids against a base full of maniacs and killer dinosaurs."

But Zoe held up a hand to shush him, staring at Keera. The pterosaur was swinging her massive head from side to side. An agitated chittering noise built in her throat and echoed around the high walls of the warehouse.

Adam eyed her worriedly. "What do you reckon's up with her?

The Z. dactyl scuttled toward them, claws clacking on the cold concrete floor of the warehouse like some nightmare monster. Then she turned toward the exit and emitted the low chittering sound again.

"Something's out there," said Zoe.

A little wobbly after doing so little for so long, Adam got up from the makeshift bed. He helped Zoe to stand, trying not to stare at the baggy material her artificial leg should've filled, and helped her over to join Keera at the broken doors. The day outside was dazzling, and Adam had to shield his eyes against the blinding glare of sunlight reflected on the vast, snowy landscape.

His face soon turned to ice in the chilled wind. The warehouse overlooked a small village—little more than a few dozen low-rise buildings dwarfed by the imposing, snow-capped mountains. There were no signs of life—but then, Adam supposed, it was seven o'clock in the morning in the Arctic. Unless it was actually seven o'clock back in Maryland, and something else altogether here. Did the sun set at all this far north?

Suddenly Keera gave a groaning gasp. She keeled over, dipping her head so she could strike the flesh above her right eye with a taloned claw, her wings rustling as if she too were shivering.

Adam frowned. "Uh . . . is she okay?"

"Duh." Zoe was peering at the giant pterosaur in concern. "I . . . I think there's something wrong with her head."

Keera released an earsplitting screech. Adam and Zoe covered their ears as a large, shimmering shadow fell over them, blotting out the sunlight overhead. Adam turned instinctively . . .

And the world seemed to slow.

There was something like a dark green dragon circling high above them—its tail a scaly coil, gnarled wings scything the air, its giant, brutish head dominated by jaws that could crunch through a truck in a single bite.

The creature swooped down toward them.

13 FAR NORTH REUNION

No, it can't be . . . Awe, excitement, disbelief—they tugged Adam's insides in all different directions.

Keera's wings knifed into flight as she propelled herself up onto the roof of the warehouse. "Adam, we've got to *move*!" yelled Zoe. "It's a Z. rex."

"The *first* Z. rex," Adam corrected her. "It's Zed!" He waved his arms above his head as the beast loomed larger in the sky, more lithe than the menaces at the hangar, less grotesque. "He's found me! Zed's found me!"

The giant figure dropped the last hundred yards and landed heavily, skidding through the icy wastes like a scaly tank out of control. Finally he came to a halt and lay there, flanks rising and falling, foam flecking his huge lips, his dark eyes barely open. He looked completely exhausted.

A mournful, keening note escaped Keera's jaws like an omen of bad things to come.

"Wait here," Adam told Zoe, breaking into a run to get to the fallen figure.

"Like I can do anything else!" Zoe shot back as she overbalanced and fell into the snow. "You're crazy! If you die, Adam, I swear, I—" Her threat was drowned out by a rooftop screech from Keera as Adam fought to clear a path through the thick-packed snow, struggling to reach the beast he'd never imagined seeing again. "Zed." He rubbed snow against the animal's sticky lips, ignoring the size and strength of those ivory teeth. "Zed, what's happened?" He paused, suddenly afraid. "It . . . it is you, isn't it?"

"Ad . . . am." The sandpaper growl lit a torch inside Adam; it was just as he remembered. But something was wrong. As he stared past Adam, only coldness shone there.

Then Adam realized Zed's baleful gaze was locked on Keera, who had dropped down from the warehouse roof. Keera threatened the newcomer with a guttural snarl, her eyes glinting with danger.

Zed struggled up, and before Adam could try and stop him, he had pounced toward the pterosaur. Landing with surprising agility he lashed out with his tail, swiping at Keera's throat. Keera dipped her head to block the blow, but the force of the strike sent her reeling backward, howling with pain.

"Adam, help me!" Zoe screamed as Keera stumbled perilously close to her prostrate body.

"Stop it, Zed!" Adam yelled as he half ran, half skidded through the churned-up snow. While Zed and Keera backed off and sized each other up, he grabbed Zoe under the arms and hauled her away into the warehouse, slipping and panting hard as he did so. "Zed, Keera's a friend . . ."

But Zed wasn't listening. He was attacking again, biting at Keera's sinewy body. The pterosaur screeched.

Ignoring the danger, Adam left Zoe and ran over to where Keera lay helpless, her vast, leathery wings flailing about. "Zed!" Adam bellowed to make himself heard above the cacophony of roars and snarls. "It's Keera. She's on our side. *Just stop!*"

Incredibly, his words had an effect. Zed halted the attack, twisting his massive head in Adam's direction. "Friend . . ." The word left its mouth in a blast of bad-tasting air—Adam felt the force of it, even several yards away.

"Yes, Keera's our friend, Zed. You mustn't attack her!"

"Ad . . . am. Danger," came the faltering reply.

He thought he was saving me. Adam glanced at Keera, who had gathered her wings together as if hugging herself; she seemed shaken but unharmed.

"OMG, he speaks." Zoe had sat up in the doorway,

staring in fearful wonder. "He really *can* talk. And he's so big! Jeez, those teeth . . . He could kill us in a second."

"But he won't." Adam looked up at the panting giant. "Zed, where've you been? Since you left, last summer—"

"Hunt. Hide." Zed snorted. "Live."

"You can't have been hanging around here?"

"Long . . . time . . . follow . . . ing . . . you." Zed inclined his great head. "Watching."

Adam wasn't sure he'd heard right. "You've been watching *me*?"

"My kind . . . take. Take people."

"You mean the kidnappings. You heard about them?"

"Not take . . . Ad . . . am." Zed nodded. "Watching . . . out."

"No way! He came to you?" Zoe was shaking her head, incredulous. "But, Adam, you flew out to Washington from Edinburgh, and you were only there two nights before Keera carried us off here . . ."

Zed glared at her and she fell silent. "Rode . . . other . . . plane," he grunted. "Hard. Hard to . . . follow."

"And as soon as you got there, I took off again," Adam murmured.

"Not save you." Zed looked away. "Slow."

"You got here, didn't you?" Adam stared at Zed's terrifying teeth, at the deadly claws and sheer brute power his frame embodied. And still a part of him wanted to reach out and hug Zed, to thank him and pet him like a loyal dog who'd returned to protect his master. *But Zed's no soppy pet who'll roll over for a bit of affection,* he reminded himself. *You saw him with Keera—he's aggressive, dangerous.*

But never with me. Adam walked up to Zed and gently pressed his palm against the dinosaur's side. "Thank you," he whispered. "Just . . . thanks. I'm so glad you're here." For the first time in so long, despite the weirdness of the situation, he actually felt safe.

Zed snorted softly but said nothing.

Then suddenly Keera started scrabbling around on the ice, swaying from side to side, the same agitated movements he'd seen back in the warehouse.

"Did Zed hurt her?" Adam wondered.

"I don't see anything." Zoe shrugged helplessly. "But something isn't right with her."

"She and Zed must both be exhausted after coming so far." Adam shivered with the cold. "I wonder how much farther we have to go."

"To the Geneflow base?" Zoe looked dubious. "We'll have to work it out. They'll have a dinosaur army there."

"Not if it's away smashing down other world landmarks," Adam pointed out. "We can at least try and check it out. Anyway, you don't know Zed. He's programmed for loads of stuff—cracking pass codes, setting explosives. He's like the James Bond of dinosaurs."

"And he looks ready to drop." Zoe managed to pull

herself up to lean in the splintered doorway. "I know you want to go charging off to try and do something, Adam. I do too. But this is big-time serious."

"Zed will watch out for us. And Keera fought off three Z. rexes before."

"So it's all right for them to fight for us? Maybe die for us?"

"No. They won't. I mean . . ." Adam realized he was trying his hardest to convince himself that they stood a chance, as well as Zoe. If he thought about things too hard, he might wimp out, and what would any of them do then? "Look, we can't just do nothing, can we? Z. animals heal quickly. Zed and Keera will be back to full strength soon."

Zoe nodded curtly. "So meantime, while they rest, how about we try preparing for the next stage of the trip? For a start, if I could find something to use as a crutch I'd be less of a liability to you."

"You're right." Adam realized how that sounded. "Not about being a liability—I mean the bit about preparing, you're right—"

"Yeah, yeah, whatever." Zoe smiled at him. "So for starters, I'll go through the food and work out how we can ration it, while you find me a big stick. Deal?"

Adam half smiled and nodded. "Deal."

Sticks were not exactly plentiful in the snowy wilderness, but Adam did find some large planks of wood in the warehouse, stacked under a tarpaulin. He carried one to a far corner where Zed lay huddled, crunching sullenly on Keera's leftovers. The Z. dactyl herself had refused to come inside; Adam hoped nobody would spot her out there. Oldman's troops would surely be hunting Keera; she knew enough to blow Geneflow's security sky-high.

He looked out through the doorway. *No chance of spotting Keera,* he realized uneasily. *'Cause she's not there.* He dropped the plank and peered outside. There was no sign of her.

"Keera's gone," he called to Zoe, who sat on the other side of the derelict space going through the food and drink.

"She'll be back," Zoe told him.

"How do you know? If we lose her now, we'll never find Dad or—"

"She'll be *back.*"

Fine. What do I know about it? Sullenly, Adam came back in and dragged the plank over to Zed. "Uh . . . can you help me cut this down a bit? Zoe needs a crutch to help her walk."

Zed eyed him and went on chewing.

"A crutch, yeah?" Adam tried again. "Zoe's a friend. We need to help her."

A low grumble sounded in the giant's scaly throat.

"If it helps, I've got something for him," Zoe called.

Adam jogged over and saw she had already grouped the food and drink into separate piles. He was still hungry and keen to fill his face, but supposed rationing made sense.

Zoe patted a pile she'd made of all the raw and frozen meat Keera had grabbed on her shoplifting spree—burgers, chops, joints. "For Zed."

"Gone in one gulp," Adam observed.

"It's meant as an offering. A gift to show I accept he's the alpha male in our pack." She shrugged. "It might encourage him to look out for me. Some modern animals do a similar thing in the wild."

"It might, yeah. How come you're so smart?"

Zoe smiled sweetly. "I didn't waste my life playing video games."

"When I've finished this crutch for you, watch I don't kick it away." Adam carried the meat back to Zed and dropped the lot in front of him. "Here you go. Zoe wants you to have this."

With a snuffling snort, Zed pushed his head forward and wolfed down the lot, packaging and all. He licked his lips, then settled back down again.

Adam pushed the plank forward with his foot. Zed reached out with a clawed finger and sliced the top of the plank clean away.

"Seemed to do the trick, Zoe," called Adam. "Uh . . . you got anything to draw with over there?"

"No."

"I was afraid of that." Grimacing, he used a shard of bone and some bear blood to scrawl the rough outline of a crutch onto the plank, wider at the top and narrower at the bottom.

Zed grunted understanding, and with slow, steady movements began to carve. Wiping his fingers on his thermal coat, Adam stared with queasy fascination. It still freaked him to see an animal so alien imitate human actions.

"Ad . . . lar . . ." Zed breathed. "Gone?"

"Dad's been taken, yeah." Adam played the voice mail yet again.

"Mur . . . mansk." The giant paused. "Four-four-seven miles . . . from here."

Is that all? Adam sighed. *Guess it's better than thousands.* "We think Keera can take us to the base."

Zed snorted, pushed the makeshift crutch aside and slumped forward as if in a sulk.

"I guess you've finished, huh?" Adam carefully picked up the hunk of wood; it fit under his arm, and they were similar heights. It was heavy, but hopefully it would do.

He took it over to Zoe, who by now sat in the middle of a sleeping bag, hacking clumsily at the fabric with a penknife. Her fingers couldn't hold the blade so well, but she kept stubbornly trying. "Hey," she said, smiling as she saw Zed's handiwork, "not bad."

"It'll give you splinters," he warned her, "but it might just work."

She scrambled up with his help and leaned on the crutch experimentally. "It'll work! Fantastic. This jacket's so padded it'll stop it digging in." She dropped back down to the sleeping bag. "And once I've made some mittens out of this thing, I'll be protected from frostbite *and* splinters."

"Sleeping-bag mittens, right. I saw Bear Grylls do the same thing on the Discovery Channel once." The feeble joke did little to lift Adam's spirits as he sat down beside her, sticking his hands in his pockets. "It's like another planet here. So cold and deserted."

Zoe nodded. "And cut off from the outside world."

"Apart from my phone with the internet on it, duh." Adam called up the browser, hoping he had enough credit to connect. Who knew how much data cost to download here. He typed *news dinosaur monster* into the search engine.

Slowly, the results came through. The headlines made for depressing reading. It seemed there had been sightings of dinosaur creatures all over the world—and many sites were linking them to the attacks on the White House, Westminster—and the destruction of the Israeli parliament. Pterosaurs had been sighted over Moscow and Beijing. Conspiracy theorists were blaming the appearance of these impossible animals on everything from flying saucers to mass hallucinations caused by nerve gas. The British and Israeli prime ministers, and many European heads of state, were flying out to emergency meetings in Washington to share information; China and the Russian Federation had not been invited.

"Getting anything?" Zoe asked.

"No," Adam lied, putting the phone away. *Why upset her as well as myself?* "I can't stop thinking about Colonel Oldman and Dr. Marrs playing us for suckers like that."

"They were so convincing," Zoe admitted. "But think about it. Oldman brought my mum to New Jersey, and Dr. Marrs brought your dad to the Pentagon. Once they had Keera, they used her as an excuse to bring all their targets together under one roof."

"You mean they could kidnap Dad and Eve and kill Keera at the same time." Adam shook his head, sickened. But however much the facts seemed to fit, he just couldn't quite believe it was true.

A heavy impact outside jolted Adam alert. He spun round—to find Keera had returned.

"Told you," said Zoe.

Three fresh-killed walruses were crushed up inside Keera's long beak. Slowly, almost waddling, she dragged her kills over to Zed, spat them out, then retreated, keeping her head close to the ground.

"Your trick again." Adam turned to Zoe, almost dumbstruck. "Did you get the idea from Keera?"

Smiling faintly, Zoe shrugged. "Or maybe Keera got it from me?"

Zed accepted the meal without even a glance at Keera, sinking his teeth deep into the carcasses. The disgusting squelching noises didn't last long; the walruses were swallowed in three greedy gulps. Then he shifted onto his side and curled his tail around himself. Keera settled in the far corner, picking at her wings with her beak, grooming herself with quiet chittering noises.

"Looks like we're one big happy family," Adam muttered. "Now, when Zed's ready, I think we should get moving."

"Then I'd better get finishing my new fashion range. Ta-da." Zoe modeled one ragged-cut mitten, her left hand stuffed between the lining's inner and outer layer. "Tie some of the loose thread round the wrist, and it should stay on okay. What do you think?"

"I think I could do with a pair of those for the journey myself." He picked up the scissors and attacked the thick fabric. "What's for tea tonight?"

"Crackers and cold baked beans."

"Ugh. Any leftover polar bear?"

Adam kept up the forced humor, hoping to distract himself from the ordeal that lay ahead. Night might not fall here in the land of the midnight sun, but still he could feel the darkness closing in.

14 OVER THE EDGE

If I live through this, thought Adam, *I won't leave school to be a dressmaker.* He had just hacked eyeholes in two of the several sleeping bags Keera had liberated from who knew where. Now if he and Zoe wore sleeping bags over their heads, they'd be able to see out. And if they wore another sleeping bag over their lower halves, they'd have full body protection from the elements. Zero points for style, but it might help them survive the freezing flight ahead.

Four-hundred-odd miles—Zed should be able to cover that in six or seven hours, Keera probably less. Adam looked at the two incredible, magnificent creatures, both sleeping soundly on the warehouse floor, and felt a growing sense of anticipation.

"We're packed and good to go," Zoe announced from behind him.

Adam turned to find her hobbling closer with the crutch, dragging yet another sleeping bag behind her with all their food and drink inside.

"You look like a low-budget Santa." Adam held up the sleeping bags he'd butchered. "Put these on. Much better look."

Zoe struggled into the sleeping bags with some difficulty. Adam was wondering if it was okay to offer her help when Keera burst awake, her wings snapping open, a cry escaping her bloodstained beak. Zed's eyes opened, and in seconds, he was on his colossal feet, tail sweeping behind him, claws raised and ready to fight. But Keera was shaking her huge head again, hitting it against the floor and clawing at the flesh above her eyes.

"She's not getting better," Zoe murmured, abandoning the upper half of her insulation to peer properly at Keera. "I thought you said Z. animals healed quickly?"

"They're supposed to," said Adam, disquieted. He looked at Zed, whose dark eyes seemed brighter, trained on Keera and missing nothing.

But as quickly as the fit had come, it seemed over. The pterosaur shook her wings, placed her head on the floor just inside the warehouse doorway, beak pointing at Zoe. Then she opened her jaws.

Zoe sucked in her cheeks. "What an invite."

"Looks like Keera's ready to go." Adam turned to Zed. "Are . . . are *you* ready? I know it could be dangerous."

The low, rumbling growl in Zed's throat signaled some kind of agreement. The huge beast stepped forward, bent over and scooped up Adam in his arms. Then he grunted at Keera, as if to say, *Got a problem with that?*

Adam held very still, aware how close he was to the steely prongs of Zed's claws. "Uh, Zed, I'd love to go with you. Let me just get my layers on first, huh?" He looked at Zoe. "You'd better put on the other bag so her saliva doesn't put you to sleep."

Zoe nodded and let him pull it over her head and shoulders. When she was tightly wrapped, he helped her shuffle across to Keera's glistening mouth. The stench of blood and raw meat made Adam hold his breath.

"Isn't this cozy?" With Adam's help, Zoe managed to drag herself inside the gooey space. "Guess there's room for the food too."

"Don't eat it all at once." Adam put the bag of provisions in beside her followed by the crutch. "Good luck."

"Yeah. And you."

Keera's jaws swung all but closed, letting air in through the bars of her sharp, spiky teeth.

While Adam clambered into his own sleeping bags, Zed hunched forward. There was a wet crunching sound, like a car popping its hood, and then the familiar gnarled, stubby wings peeled out from his back.

Once Adam had positioned the bag's eyeholes over his

head so he could see out, he stood with his back toward Zed and held up his arms. "Here we go, then . . ."

Zed wrapped his arms around Adam—it was like being hugged by two overfed boa constrictors. Squashed up against the dinosaur's tough, scaly hide, Adam tried to keep calm as he was carried to the doorway in a few loping strides—and then, the sickening rush of takeoff was rearranging both heart and stomach.

Oh, my God . . .

The speed of their ascent, combined with the icy chill of the wind, took Adam's breath away. It was freezing cold out here, raw and uncomfortable. And yet as they rose higher and higher into the blue, Adam couldn't help but let loose a whooping cheer of exhilaration. He glanced to his right and saw Keera had quickly caught up, wings spread wide, powering through the air beside them.

The warehouse—their shelter and respite from the arctic wilds—was lost from sight in seconds. Now there was only the rolling wilderness.

Adam had gone flying with Zed in his dreams so many times, but the anticipated sense of joy and freedom soon faded. So much had changed since he and Zed had shared their first adventure. Back then, it had been the two of them alone, simply trying to find and rescue his father. Now the stakes had risen to the max. Governments of the world were involved with the Geneflow menace—and it seemed that corruption and betrayal ran to the very top.

Adam stared down at frozen lakes and snowbound forests as the landscape blurred by. He wondered how Zoe was feeling, unable to walk or fend for herself. What was his dad doing right now? How was he feeling? What about Eve—was she okay?

But the question that hammered hardest in his head was as big as it was simple: *What are Geneflow really planning?* If their base was in Russia, perhaps Marrs and Oldman had been telling the truth about Geneflow accepting Russian money in exchange for . . . what? For all he knew, Geneflow's scientists had thousands of dinosaurs waiting to unleash yet more havoc and devastation on the world.

The questions nagged, while the answers kept their distance, out of reach.

The bitter arctic winds swept them over the tundra. As Zed flew raggedly onward, Keera matched his pace. After a time, it started to snow, and Adam moved his face away from the eyeholes to avoid the stinging blizzard. He grew tired and sore in his insulated prison. His thoughts turned to longings for water, for a cooked meal or a change of clothes.

After at least an eternity, Zed abruptly climbed higher into the sky. Heart jumping, Adam looked out ahead through his peephole. Barren mountains formed a partition between here and the horizon. But as he was lifted over the peaks, the view opened up into something incredible. Below, the mountains fell away sharply into a spectacular canyon as wide as a freeway and who knew how deep, its bottom lost in freezing fog. Level with the mountaintops on the other side of the sheer drop was a bleak plateau, its boundaries blurred by the mist . . .

Keera gave a sharp warning cry and blurred into stealth mode. Moments later, Zed had followed suit. Adam wished *he* could turn invisible too, because below, in the center of the plateau, he spied a clutch of concrete skyscrapers surrounded by smaller buildings—a drab, boxy town.

Oh, my God, is that it—the Geneflow base?

But even from here, Adam could see something was wrong. The streets, sidewalks and offices were all empty. *Where are all the cars? Where are the people?*

It was a ghost town.

Abruptly, Zed veered away from the buildings and circled down with Adam toward the edge of the canyon, where a stretch of higher ground shielded the creepy city from their view. As he landed with a jolting lurch in the thick snow, Zed turned visible once more. He placed Adam down a little too close to the canyon's edge for his liking; snow swirled in a wild flurry as the wind whipped it over the edge.

"We'll have to get closer to that ghost town," Adam announced, struggling out of his thick fabric shroud. "Zed, Dad and Eve might be being held in one of those buildings. They'll probably be wearing antistink, but . . . can you get any scent?"

Zed sniffed the air, then snorted, shook his head. He seemed distracted and was looking all around, alert, his tail twitching.

"What's up?" Adam asked.

Suddenly Keera shimmered back into sight, gliding in to land close by. She touched down gracefully despite her huge size, and moments later, her jaws yawned wide to reveal Zoe. The girl had already pulled her sleeping bag from her head and shoulders and now struggled out from inside. With the crutch gripped in her swaddled hands, trailing her other sleeping bag like a fantastical tail, she looked dirtier and more disheveled than ever. Adam hurried to help her up, but she waved his arm away; he left her to it and got the food and drink instead, pulling out some Sunny D and gulping it down. He wasn't normally a fan, but after hours of thirsting in the air, it tasted fantastic.

As Zoe finally managed to stand with the help of the crutch, he passed her the bottle. She drank deeply while he liberated some breadsticks from the bag.

"Where'd you and Keera get to?" he asked, crunching noisily.

"She took me in for a closer look at that ghost town," Zoe explained, pulling off her mitt and grabbing a breadstick herself. "There's an airstrip on the far side of those skyscrapers, and it's been cleared of snow."

"Someone's used it recently." Adam felt nerves spark in his guts. "Someone must have been flown in!"

Zoe nodded as she ate. "No sign of anyone living there, though. It's weird. Most of the buildings are the same style, and kind of run down."

"So?"

"Well, towns and cities sort of change over time, don't they? New bits are added on, old bits are built over." Zoe shivered in the cold and grabbed another bread stick. "This place looks like it was all built in one go and no one's come back since."

"Apart from whoever was on that plane." Adam saw that Zed was still jumpy, looking all around, and found himself doing the same.

"Hey, is that a cave?" Zoe pointed out a round shadow in the snowy sweep of the nearest hillside. "We should probably stay out of sight while we work out what we do next."

"Anywhere we can shelter has got to be good." Adam peered more closely at the opening, which was maybe fifty yards away and half hidden by snow. "Should be room for Zed and Keera too—"

But then Keera made a low, eerie chittering noise in the back of her throat, a sound that spoke of danger. With her hopping, birdlike gait, she closed the distance to the cave in seconds.

And then something large and gray burst out in an explosion of snow. The violent movement sent Keera clattering upward into startled flight. Zed roared in warning, and Zoe caught hold of Adam's arm as a clay-gray creature almost twice their size pushed out from the icy space inside. Stubby metallic quills sprouted from its shoulders and torso. The reptile snarled and snapped its jaws as it stood in the cave entrance.

Weak with terror, Adam recognized it in a heartbeat. *Utahraptor!* He'd been hunted by crude, vicious Brutes like this on Raptor Island.

Before he could yell out any kind of warning, Keera descended with a nerve-scraping screech, legs kicking at the scaly monster, driving it back inside the cave. But a second Brute jumped out from inside and bit deep into her left wing. Zoe screamed as four more of the clay-gray monsters emerged and set about her like rats attacking a cat, snapping and tearing at her flesh with a terrifying bloodlust. Keera's yowls were drowned out by the barking, snapping pack of Brutes as they hauled her inside the cave.

Mercifully, Adam's view was blocked as Zed stood in front of him and Zoe, a vast, scaly shield. He was so much bigger than the raptors. In the natural way of things, they'd never dare attack.

But these creatures weren't remotely natural.

As the bloodied Brutes scuttled out from inside the cave—six, seven, more, maybe—they broke instantly in a charge for Zed, jaws wide and stretched back to reveal their carving-knife teeth to full effect.

"Get us out of here, Zed!" Adam shouted. "Those things spit acid! If you get too close—"

Too late. The Brutes were already spraying thick jets of liquid. Adam threw himself at Zoe, knocking her into the snow as the rain of acid fell around it.

Zed's face was the target. The towering dinosaur bellowed with pain and staggered back—almost crushing Adam as he did so—clawing at his eyes, swinging his head all about in a gruesome, agonized dance.

"No!" Adam yelled helplessly.

"We've got to hide," sobbed Zoe, clawing at the snow, trying to bury herself. "Help me!"

But Adam couldn't move, transfixed by the animal violence. Fearless, the first two Brutes had hurled themselves at Zed, biting and clawing. Zed quickly batted them away, but they simply attacked again—and, blinded by the acid attack, he couldn't see that they were driving him dangerously close to the precipice.

Zed pushed out his wings ready to fly to safety, but now the other Brutes were attacking in force, a writhing mass of teeth, claws and muscle. Four pounced onto his back, biting and gouging at the gristly sails, gripping him around the neck so he couldn't beat his wings. Others clawed at his legs and belly, circling and snapping, relentless, forcing him backward.

The struggle was over in seconds. Roaring impotently, Zed floundered over the edge of the chasm, the Brutes clinging to his struggling form even as they went to their deaths.

"No!" Adam screamed.

Zoe twisted hard on his arm. "Shhh!"

But, alerted by Adam's cry, one of the six remaining Brutes whirled round. Its eyes narrowed at the sight of easy prey. The rest of the pack turned as one and began to advance—gibbering, hissing and hungry for the kill.

But with the pierce of a siren, a new screech rose above the Brutes' roars. Adam's eyes snapped open to find Keera attacking the Brutes from behind. Her wings were raked with cuts and steaming with acid burns, but like some hideous angel of death, she had risen again—to deal a brutal retribution.

The claws of one foot hooked down into a Brute's eyes and yanked its head back so far its neck snapped in a moment. Another Brute howled as her jaws crunched down on its arm, ripping the limb away at the shoulder. It flailed about in gory panic, smashing its pack brothers aside while Keera flapped out of reach of the acid sprays fired in retaliation. Moments later, she dived back down behind her attackers and opened their backs with her talons. As they shrieked with pain and anger, Keera stretched her wings as wide as she could and swept the wounded animals clear over the precipice. Their terrified shrieks lingered in the air, but the Brutes themselves were already lost in the white soup of snow and fog.

Keera circled over the chasm like a giant bird of prey, blood streaming from her wounds, her body mottled black with bruises. She shrieked her defiance into the void before landing with a stumble back on the snowy ledge. The battle and the bloodshed had ended with the same swift ferocity as it had begun.

Still stunned, Adam stumbled over to Keera. “Are you okay? My God, Keera, that was the bravest thing I ever . . . I mean, you were . . .” The words trailed off as he looked past her to the precipice. Surely, any moment now, Zed would come soaring up to join them, recovered.

“Zed!” he called, trudging over to the ledge, where he fell to his knees. He waited and waited, the bitter wind bringing tears to his eyes. There was nothing to see.

A hand came down on his shoulder. He turned to see Zoe had dragged herself through the snow to join him. Shaking clods of icy white from her hair and shoulders, she put her arms around Adam and began to sob.

Then both were thrown aside as the air exploded into fierce blue sparks around Keera. The pterosaur’s scream sounded almost human as she shook in a haze of indigo. *Electroshock weapons,* Adam realized numbly. *Geneflow’s found us.* He tried to see Keera’s attackers, but the glare was too great. “Zoe, we’ve got to run,” he hissed. “I’ll carry you, come on.”

But Zoe didn’t seem to hear, clutching her head as if feeling the pain herself. “Leave her alone! You’re killing her.”

Finally the electric onslaught cut out and Keera crumpled, lifeless, to the ground. She was so battered and beaten, Adam couldn’t look at her. While Zoe went on kneeling and clutching her head, Adam held up his hands in surrender as four people closed in, their features masked by hoods and scarves and snow goggles, each carrying a large, tubular weapon.

Fear gave Adam courage, and he lunged for the nearest gun, hoping to wrestle it free. But he slipped in the snow and fell beside Zoe. A boot smacked into his ribs, and he gasped. The figures loomed over him, shock weapons pointed at his head.

"No. Don't harm him." It was a woman's voice.

The circle of guards parted to reveal a figure, dressed in a padded fur-trimmed parka, hat and goggles. "Hello, Adam. Hello, Zoe. Thank you for coming."

Her? Adam recognized the voice, but didn't want to. *It's impossible. She's dead.*

"All our raptor sentries—destroyed? The death of this rogue pterosaur really is long overdue." The woman pulled off her fur-lined hat and goggles to reveal dark, striking and all-too-familiar features.

"Samantha Josephs . . ." Adam felt winded. She looked just the same as when he'd first met her—and yet he'd seen her mauled to death by one of her own creations. "How? I saw you die on Raptor Island."

"Try to use your intelligence." Josephs's tone was a good match for the freezing arctic air. "*I* have never been to Raptor Island."

Adam was reeling with shock. "But then how—"

"I was cloned from Samantha Josephs almost a year

ago. One of us may be dead, but the other goes on." The woman took a menacing step closer. "Blind luck has allowed your survival when the odds would seem against it, but science has made *me* immortal. And science will beat chance every time." She looked at him almost pityingly. "I will never die, Adam, but very soon now, your world will perish."

15 TAKING A LIFE

Finally, Adam understood Josephs's last words to him on Raptor Island, spat through bleeding lips: *It's all right. I'm still alive . . . You haven't even won yourself breathing space.*

"There's really no call for such a dumbstruck expression." Josephs's English accent lent a glass-sharp edge to her words. "You're an intelligent child. You know we have cloned many animals; you have seen how we can download human minds into computers and upload them into new bodies—"

"But you're exactly the same." Adam's voice was hoarse. "I thought a clone of a person would have to grow from, like, a baby."

"The cells of the clone are force-evolved, expertly

matured until they match the original. Then we transfer all memories, experience and personality to create a perfect duplicate." Josephs shrugged as if this were picture-book simple. "When Jeffrey Hayden was killed by your pet Z. rex, Geneflow lost its director of operations needlessly. So, when I took over his position, my first act was to step up our research into human replication."

"Where's my dad," Adam broke in, "and Zoe's mum?"

"All in good time." Josephs looked at Zoe, who was still rocking on her haunches, sobbing quietly. "I suggest you both come inside before you die of exposure." She turned to two of the guards. "Take them to the Neural Suite."

One of the guards hauled Adam to his feet by the scruff of his neck.

Zoe struggled as another picked her up from the ground. "What are you going to do with Keera?"

"The beast will be recycled," said Josephs simply, turning to the other two guards. "See to it—then get over to the airstrip, ready to greet the new arrivals. There are two more planes due to land today."

"Keera!" As the guard trudged away toward the Brutes' cave, Zoe twisted in his arms, staring helplessly at the broken body of Keera, lying abandoned in the crimson snow. Gloved fingers dug into Adam's neck and marched him forward after her.

Josephs didn't mention Zed, Adam realized. *If he's still alive in the canyon there—and he's* got *to be—he'll come after us. He'll save us. He'll . . .* But as he passed Keera, all bloodied and burned, hope began to fade. In the hillside opening, he saw three snowmobiles waiting. *It's not a cave at all—it's the mouth of a tunnel.*

The two guards loaded Zoe and Adam on board the nearest Ski-Doo. Josephs climbed into the one behind, while the other two guards remained with Keera. Then, with a throaty roar, the powerful sleds started off down the icy passageway.

Dim lights shone overhead as they passed huge nests made from trampled rubbish, piles of bones, stinking dung heaps. Other tunnels fed into the passage on both sides. "It's like an underground burrow," Adam realized. "The raptors live out here on guard. There must be exits all around the city so they can come out and kill unwelcome visitors."

"We never stood a chance," was Zoe's only response.

Adam tried to remember the twists and turns they took through the wide tunnels, dismayed by just how deep and far they seemed to be going.

Finally, the vehicles slowed down as they reached a large underground parking area. A huge, rusty metal goods elevator was built into a rocky wall, shielded by two sets of sliding doors. Josephs got out of her Ski-Doo and crossed to it.

Adam's captor forced him out of the snowmobile and marched him across to join her. "Are we under the city?" Adam asked.

"That's right." Josephs pressed a complicated series of buttons on a keypad beside the doors, and they cranked slowly open.

"Did Colonel Oldman and Dr. Marrs tell you we'd be coming?" Adam was pushed into the scuffed steel space inside. "We know they're working for Geneflow."

"Actually, they're not," said Josephs casually. "And Zoe's mother isn't here either, I'm afraid."

Adam swapped frowns with Zoe. "What?"

"We asked Bill Adlar to *say* all that so you wouldn't look to Fort Meade for help." She smiled at Adam. "You'd come to us instead. Of course, that meant hacking into your phone and blocking all calls save for ours—"

"Then, the colonel and Dr. Marrs *are* on our side . . . ?" Adam felt as if the mental bolts that held him together were coming undone. He bowed his head. "Dad lied. You *made* him lie. What did you do to him—?"

"Let me go!" Suddenly Zoe bucked and twisted in the arms of her guard. "I'm not going anywhere with you!"

"Use some logic, Zoe," said Josephs. "If you were released without support or a wheelchair, how could you hope to get away in any case?"

Zoe stopped struggling and glared at Josephs, close to tears. "All we've been through. All the pain. I thought, at least at the end of it, I'll see Mum . . ."

Josephs said nothing, but once Zoe's guard had carried her in and closed the doors, she pressed a red button. The elevator started downward, rumbling and rattling. Deeper and deeper underground they went. Adam saw Zoe's eyes glinting with tears. If he hadn't felt so absolutely numb, he might've joined in.

"I want to see my dad," he muttered.

"You will, in due course," said Josephs briskly.

"Where is this place, anyway?"

"In the early nineteen eighties, when the Cold War between East and West was coldest, the former Soviet Union built dozens of underground cities. Elaborate shelters in which the privileged few could survive a nuclear war." Josephs unzipped her heavy coat as the elevator continued its plunge into the earth. "Towns like the one above, closed to the public, housed the construction workers as they toiled below and made a good cover for what they'd been doing here. As the global situation improved for a time, the cities were abandoned. Now *we* have acquired them."

"So the military's right," Adam breathed, "Russia *has* taken control of Geneflow."

Josephs smiled as if at some secret joke. "It would seem so. Wouldn't it?"

Finally the elevator lurched to a stop and the doors clanked open onto dim lights and cinder blocks. Adam and Zoe were taken after Josephs as she walked smartly into a nondescript corridor. A man came into sight at the end of the corridor, balding with a wispy beard.

"I've checked the raptors' life signs," he called in an accent that sounded French, not Russian. "They're dead. All our sentries, dead!"

Josephs nodded as she closed the distance between them. "The beast responsible is being recycled."

Beast singular, thought Adam as the guards stopped their herding, waiting for their mistress to move on. *She can't have seen Zed then, before he . . .*

"Don't kill Keera," Zoe said quietly. "Please."

Josephs spared her the briefest of glances. "Have the labs grow new sentries, Mr. Thierry."

Thierry looked doubtful. "We're at full capacity rearing Z. rexes for the attack on Mongolia."

"That takes precedence," Josephs agreed.

"With Russia to their north and China to their south, they'll join the West in blaming one of them—"

"Yes. Tensions must continue to rise. Carry on, Mr. Thierry." Josephs turned from him and resumed her brisk walk. Thierry spared a brief, puzzled glance at Adam, Zoe and their captors as they pushed past, but said nothing more.

The cinder-block corridors seemed to stretch on for miles, but Josephs finally stopped beside a set of double doors and swiped a pass card through an electronic reader on the wall. The doors opened stiffly onto a large, shadowy room. As the guards pushed Adam and Zoe inside, a series of strip lights on the ceiling flickered into life with dazzling brightness.

Adam blinked away his blindness and, with a sick feeling of dread, realized the room was some kind of operating theater. Restraint straps dangled from a cushioned table in the center of the room. A huge, rectangular slab of glass and metal hung down from the ceiling above it, like a giant flatbed scanner turned upside down.

And beside the table, Adam saw a stainless-steel trolley with a collection of scalpels and scary-looking instruments. Panicking, he kicked and struggled for release with manic determination. But the men held him fast, in silence.

"Don't distress yourself, Adam." Josephs removed her coat and placed it on a chair. "Zoe will be first."

"No!" Zoe shrieked as the guards manhandled her onto the cushioned table and held her down while Josephs secured the heavy straps over her arms and chest, her thighs and her forehead. "Please, don't!"

"What are you doing?" Adam demanded.

"I'm trying to help you," Josephs told Zoe. "This process offers you a chance to live on, free from the prison of your . . . unfortunate body."

"It's not a prison." Zoe stared up at her hatefully. "It's who I am."

"'Who you are' is a stew of chemicals and blind chance," Josephs retorted. "Your life's been so limited by your physical condition, hasn't it? But then, we're all of us trapped in these inefficient bodies, doomed from birth to grow old and decay." She crossed to a computer in the corner of the lab and started it up. "Or rather, we *were*."

Adam swallowed hard, staring helplessly at Zoe as she tried not to shake. "What do you mean?"

"Einstein once said 'a new type of thinking is essential if mankind is to survive and move to higher levels.' How right he was." Josephs turned to face him. "Imagine what Einstein could have gone on to achieve if he had never died . . . or if Wagner were still composing today, or Michelangelo still painting." She smiled. "Now that we have perfected human cloning and mind transference, when an old body wears out, it can be replaced with a new one."

"So . . . if you had had my mum's mind in your computer and her DNA on file"—he stared at Josephs—"you could have made a new one after she died?"

She nodded. "Of course. But only minds worthy of preserving will go on. Great thinkers, fertile intellects. When they have so much left to give, to let them perish would be a foolish waste."

"And I suppose you get to choose who they are—" A sudden realization kicked in Adam's head. "These experts and scientists you've kidnapped . . . you're cloning them too?"

"Of course." Josephs turned back to her computer and started up some software. The glass slab hanging over Zoe glowed and hummed. Machine parts inside it swept slowly from one end to the other.

"What is that thing?" Zoe said, her voice shaking. "What's it doing?"

"It's mapping your entire body—every cell, inside and out." Josephs glanced over from the computer. "You know, you're an interesting case, Zoe. It's possible that your disability has enhanced your empathy with animals; in your heart of hearts, you see yourself like them, less than human."

"Shut up," snapped Zoe.

"It would be easy to cure your Proteus syndrome, but were we to place your mind in another body, would that empathy still flourish?"

"I said shut up! Who cares!"

"Geneflow cares." Josephs studied Zoe thoughtfully. "I'm sure Adam's told you how we placed human minds into raptor bodies."

"Sick," Adam muttered.

"Essential," Josephs countered. "Those experiments were simply a first step. Our final aim has always been to create a new kind of human-reptile hybrid." She held up a hand to silence his inevitable protest. "Of course, you reject the idea outright. You are a child—you have no concept of how important this research will prove. But the fact is, our hybrids often experience personality changes, are unable to accept their new bodies even after . . . persuasion."

"You mean you can't do their thinking for them?" Adam sneered.

Josephs took the dig seriously. "Well, we can train them using Think-Send, but . . . still the problems remain." She looked at Zoe. "I wonder how *you* would adapt. On the one hand, you would be able-bodied, but on the other—"

"People will always be people however you mess with their heads," Zoe insisted. "I mean, I'm not some stupid experiment, I'm—I'm *somebody.*" There was fear and pleading in her eyes as she gazed up at Josephs. "Please. Leave me as I am."

"With the global chain of events we've set in motion, that's not even an option. Not for any of us." From a drawer beside the computer, Josephs removed what looked like a high-tech hairnet studded with tiny electrodes. She crossed to Zoe and started fitting the net carefully to the contours of Zoe's head.

"Get off!" Zoe tried to pull away. "What are you doing?"

"Preparing the neural interface. The sensors in the net will measure and map the pathways of your brain, absorb the codings of your personality, your memories—and build a virtual reconstruction here on our hard drives."

"No," pleaded Zoe. "No . . ."

"Oh, yes." Josephs plucked a long wire from Zoe's electronic hairnet and plugged it into a kind of large metal coffin that stood against the wall. A single red light on the coffin's blank, battered face glowed to acknowledge the connection—and Zoe's entire body went limp, as if some switch inside her had been suddenly thrown.

"What have you done?" Adam whispered.

"I've placed Zoe in a state of sensory deprivation. It is necessary."

"How is *any* of this necessary?"

"A new era is beginning. I know that sounds corny, but it's true." Josephs got up, took something from the steel trolley and walked toward him. "If we are going to reboot human existence, we must wipe out all the obsolete peoples of the world and replace them with our own."

Adam struggled, but the guards' grip only tightened. "You . . . you're mad!"

She pushed her face up close to his. "You think the world as it is now is better?" she hissed. "*That* is madness."

Adam tried to think of a smart response—then gasped at a sting in his arm. As Josephs stepped back, he saw that she was holding a syringe. "What was . . . What are you . . . ?"

"The wheels are already in motion." Josephs's face began to blur and distort as whatever she'd given him spread, tangling through his bloodstream. "And you, Adam, with your Think-Send skills and the ear of the United States military, *you* are going to help to bring it about."

16 PEOPLE CAN CHANGE

Adam woke in darkness. Memories tumbled back from sleep's shadows and, with them, fear. He was strapped down; only his arms were free. He tried to touch his temples, but his fingers brushed metal; he was wearing some kind of headset, as if ready to play Ultra-Reality.

Why was I drugged? Adam scraped his tongue about his dry mouth. *Where am I now? How long's it been? Where's Zoe?* The hiss and whir of hard drives spoke of computers somewhere close by, and a faint light was stealing in from somewhere. He could just make out a clock on the wall.

It was one thirty P.M. He'd been out for hours.

Adam pawed at the fastenings of the strap around his

midriff but couldn't loosen it. "Zoe?" he hissed nervously. "Are you there?"

A rough hand clamped down over his lips.

Surprised, Adam tried to scream—then heard a familiar voice low and hoarse in his ear. "Don't. Please, Ad, stay quiet."

Adam couldn't believe it. He looked up through the dark and saw a faint silhouette. "Dad?"

"I'm so glad to see you, Ad. Now, please, they mustn't hear us."

Adam nodded his understanding.

"I didn't want to lie to you. They made me." His speech was a little slurred. "You'll feel woozy for a while. Josephs put you to sleep, but I've woken you. I wasn't supposed to, but—"

"Why did she drug me?"

"Wait. Let me make sure there's no one close by." Mr. Adlar swept aside a thick dark curtain, which partitioned Adam's couch from the rest of the room like a patient's bed in a hospital ward. The faint light had been coming from three large computer monitors set on a long workbench, half buried in wires and circuits and other high-tech clutter. Now Adam watched, heart in throat, as his father tapped at a keyboard and a window opened on the main screen, showing a view of the corridors outside.

"How did you do that?" he whispered, his throat sandpaper dry.

Mr. Adlar, staring at the screen intently, did not turn around. "I hacked into the security camera feed without anyone knowing." He was wearing a lab coat. With the tap of another key, the image changed to show the airstrip; a plane had landed, and its bundled-up passengers were handing luggage to waiting guards. Another, and the view switched to the streets above, the concrete buildings stained with decay and crumbling.

With every tap, an unpleasant new view was revealed: there was Mr. Thierry in a room crowded with televisions switched to different news feeds . . . the Neural Suite where he and Zoe had been taken, now empty . . . a strange cavernous space, piled high with the bodies of cattle and horses; some of the animals were still alive, crushed in together. With a stammer in his heart, Adam saw a Z. rex dart into the frame—not Zed. It was bigger and dull brown, like the ones sent to Patuxent. It swallowed a whole horse in one bloody bite, and as the surrounding animals scattered, limping feebly, they revealed the giant bulk of a pterosaur lying sprawled on the filthy floor.

No way, that can't be—

The picture changed as his dad clicked on. "Dad, wait," Adam hissed. "Go back!"

But his dad was busy moving the images on. The view showed the length of another bare corridor, painted white. "It's all right," he muttered. "They're not keeping tabs. Must think I'm fully under."

"Under what?" Adam was hardly listening. "Dad, go back, please," he said desperately. "That room with the animals—"

"That's where they let the Z. beasts rest between missions." Mr. Adlar tapped back the other way until he got to the cavernous concrete space again. "As you can imagine, they need a lot of feeding. Thierry has to clone livestock by the cartload to meet the appetites of those things."

"But, Dad, that's Keera in there!"

"The pterosaur, you mean?"

Adam cringed, watching the Z. dactyl twitch as bloody hooves trampled her body. "Of course, the pterosaur!"

"Must be down for recycling. Some of the creatures develop mental problems, so it's easiest to feed them back to the healthy ones. There's nothing we can do." His back still to Adam, Mr. Adlar shook his head. "The animals are herded in to be eaten alive or dropped in through the roof hatch the Z. beasts use to get in and out. Both ways are guarded. If the pterosaur isn't dead already, she soon will be."

"You're talking like you don't even know her." A thought filtered through Adam's muddled brain. "Why won't you look at me?"

Mr. Adlar let out a heavy breath. "I was never meant to speak to you. Supposed to just come in and give you the treatment like I did the others . . . like you're a stranger." He picked up a spent syringe from the workbench. "But how could I not wake you and talk with you? You're all I have left. I miss you so much every day, every single day."

Adam was starting to feel severely creeped out. "I don't get you, Dad. What are you talking about?"

Slowly, hesitantly, Mr. Adlar turned to face Adam in the dim light from the monitors. "Ad, what's on the outside doesn't matter. I . . . I know you might be scared, but I'm just the same. You must know, you heard me telling you those memories on the phone, I'm—"

"No." Adam barely croaked the word as all reason and response left his head.

In the eerie glow of the screens, he could see now: this wasn't his dad. It was a monster. The skin on that careworn, much-loved face had turned scaly, reptilian, distorting the features. The whole head was hairless, the ears and nose flattened to barely more than bumps and ridges in the thick, alien flesh.

"I've gone mad," Adam whispered, tears stinging the backs of his eyes. "This is another of Geneflow's sick stunts. I'm wearing the Ultra-Reality helmet, right? It's just another simulation—"

"It's me, Ad." The thing that sounded like his father held up scaly hands as if to calm him down. "It's Dad."

"What did they do to you?" Adam wanted to scream and shout. "I mean, they only took you a few days ago . . ."

"No, Adam. I've been here for months. I told you, Josephs made me lie to you." A deep shuddering breath in the dark, then more words, slurred and bitter. "Geneflow cloned me from a blood sample they took back in Edinburgh. While they were holding me, they mapped my mind, replicated my memories and made me into this. A half man who remembers you, loves you, even if I don't look like the man *you* care about."

Adam swallowed back bile. "They made you . . . a monster."

"Josephs calls me a pioneer of New Humanity." This half-human Adlar turned away again as if ashamed. "See, they needed me for my skill with Think-Send. But once the bulk of my duties had been performed, they made me a part of their controlled evolution program."

Adam couldn't help but stare again. "Josephs said something about making human-reptile hybrids."

"Yes." The reptile man turned to face Adam again, a harder rasp to his words. "Stronger, powerful bodies, harder to break than yours. Bodies that heal faster, that resist radiation, like the Z. beasts—so much better suited to postapocalyptic conditions."

Adam froze. "Post-*what*?" He remembered Josephs's words—*your world will perish*—and remembered the Geneflow sim that had got him into this whole mess. A landscape of endless ruins.

"The apocalypse, Adam. Total destruction."

Adam stared helplessly at the creature confronting him. "Geneflow and Russia are working together, aren't they? They're going to start World War III . . ."

"There'll be a nuclear war, yes. But Geneflow isn't working for the Russians. And Geneflow doesn't have nuclear weapons. It doesn't need them."

"Then how can they start a war . . . ?"

"Don't you see, Ad? All these high-profile attacks, on the White House, on the British and Israeli parliaments . . . the one they're planning on Mongolia's capital . . ." The half man shook his hideous head. "Geneflow has set the nations of the world at each other's throats, breeding suspicion, trying to push the planet to the brink of war."

Adam clutched at a forlorn hope. "But . . . if Russia's not to blame, there'll be no real evidence."

"That's where I come in. Me and those kidnapped experts." The reptile man looked at the floor. "Their minds have been mapped and copied, ready to be uploaded into hybrid bodies like mine. So now Geneflow can allow a few of the originals to think they've escaped—and make things even worse."

"I don't get you."

"I've Think-Sent false memories into these people's heads. Whole scenes, rendered in Ultra-Reality and placed directly in the brain." A boasting tone began to edge his words. "I've made a Russian scientist believe he's been held in secret by the CIA and a Western scientist believe he's been a prisoner of the Kremlin—" He laughed, short and hard. "That's *real* programming skill, Ad. That's game design like nothing else."

"It's horrible," Adam whispered. "They'll really believe they're telling the truth . . ."

"And as witnesses they're so well respected, their countries won't doubt them. The global situation will worsen further with accusations and counteraccusations—until someone pushes the big red button." The cloned Bill Adlar twitched. "If we're going to reboot human existence, we must wipe out all the obsolete peoples of the world and replace them with our own."

"That's not you talking; it's Josephs." Adam felt sick. "She's brainwashed you! Used my dad's—*your*—invention to make you think what she wants you to think!"

"*Homo sapiens* will be launched all over again, only this time our species will thrive by intelligent design. Think-Send will educate new humans, unite them in creating one global nation."

"Ruled by Josephs and her friends," said Adam bitterly.

"Course, it'll be at least ten years before farming and food production is possible again." The half man seemed lost in the nightmare picture he was painting. "During that decade, the Z. beasts will hunt down all survivors of the Apocalypse and kill them. The last of old humanity, gone."

"But if there's no food . . . ?"

"We clone our meat and grain here. We recycle our wastewater." The hybrid crossed to the couch and stared down at him. "Above us, the city's ready to fall, but down here, we can go on for forty years or more—sealed off from the surface and powered by our own atomic plant. Chartered planes are bringing all personnel here to sit out the nuclear winter—"

Adam had heard enough. "Great! You can all sit around playing sims for years."

"With the old world razed, we can go out and begin a better one." The hybrid smiled. "We can withstand the radioactive conditions. We can work for hours without tiring. We'll pave the way so that human beings reach their true potential, their *zenith* . . ."

As the hybrid moved away, Adam could see the security monitor again; he stared miserably at Keera's half-trampled form. And with an electric shock in his chest, he caught sight of a quilted bundle lying in the crook of one of the pterosaur's giant wings.

Oh, my God.

"Zoe!" Adam struggled uselessly against the straps that pinned him to the couch. "They've put Zoe in there! We've got to get her out. She'll be torn to pieces!"

"The Z. beasts would do the same to you." The reptile man, holding a length of wire, took a step toward him. "It's okay, Adam. In a short while now, we'll be together again."

"What are you doing?" Adam watched, skin crawling, as his cloned dad drew closer—then remembered Josephs: *A new era is beginning . . . and you, Adam, with your Think-Send skills and the ear of the United States military, you are going to help to bring it about.* "You're going to put fake evidence in *my* head too, aren't you?"

"I have to, Ad." The reptile man looked ashamed. "I've so longed to talk with you, but once you're conditioned, you'll forget all we've said. You'll only remember what we tell you to."

"Please—"

"But I still need to tell you, the only reason I've helped them is because they promised to clone you too." The creature's scaly flesh puckered in a sad smile. "Josephs just showed me the start of the process that will bring a new you into the world."

"A new me?" Adam's voice cracked with emotion. "Dad, you can't do this."

"I must." The clone sounded so tired. "Everything's prepared. Fake memories, impressions, dialogue for you to recall and pass on . . ." The half man pushed the wire into a connector on the Think-Send helmet. A pulse of energy buzzed through Adam's brain, and he gasped with pain.

"I'm . . . sorry," the half man said.

"My real dad would never hurt me." Adam swallowed the threatening tears. "He'd never settle for a different me, something fake."

"You'll be just the same, Ad."

"I'll hate you forever!"

"We can change the way you think. Make you forget what I've done." Though the reptilian skin made it hard to read emotion, gray eyes glistened as if with tears. "I lost your mother. I won't lose you too."

"Please!" Adam's voice grew higher, more urgent. "If you let me go, I could help you, warn my real dad and Oldman that—"

"Josephs would have me killed." A pause. "And I want to survive."

The thing that called itself Bill Adlar walked to the desk and curled scaly fingers around the computer mouse. Adam strained with all his strength to break free. But it wasn't enough. He realized with hard, horrid clarity that this was the end. No last-minute rescue, no friend to save him.

"Forgive me," came his father's whisper.

Adam heard the click of the mouse—and then a digital express train hurtled into his head. The slam of sound and images broke his brains like bone, and then—

17 LOOKING AT YOU

Where am I now? Adam woke sharply and flinched from the bright light. He wasn't strapped to a couch; he was lying on a kind of hospital trolley. The room was small, bare, painted white. A cracked strip light buzzed above him, and there was a door on either side of the bed. He realized he was wearing thermal gear—proper warm clothes, clean and dark, like the ones the personnel at Geneflow had worn. His phone was in his pocket, though the battery had died. He sat up. New boots, too, thick and insulated. Like he was due to go outside. Why was that? He couldn't think clearly, couldn't remember just what had—

Zoe.

Adam sat bolt upright and scrambled off the trolley.

Dizziness overwhelmed him, and he leaned heavily against the wall. He saw a clock opposite, struggled blearily to make sense of the figures. *I've got to get her out. Got to . . .*

It was coming up to five o'clock in the morning. *I've been asleep thirteen hours.*

By now, Zoe and Keera will be . . .

Closing his eyes, Adam tried not to picture what must surely have happened hours ago. He waited for tears to build, for some release to come. But there was something blocking his ordinary thoughts; a memory that sat awkwardly in his mind.

A memory of that hateful reptilian face.

"You were right about me, Ad." His father's voice, devoid of all emotion, played over the image, tinnily in his head like a voice mail message. "I started the process, but . . . I couldn't go through with it. So, I've uploaded just the basic audiovisual files, without the mental conditioning to make you believe they're real."

Even as Adam thought about this, he triggered a vivid image of Russian soldiers in green uniform, crowding around a Z. rex. *A memory of something I've never even seen.*

"You'll need this information to play along, 'cause Josephs will want to be sure her 'escaped prisoners' tell the right story to their national embassies." Mr. Adlar's voice paused. "If she guesses that you're faking it, she'll kill us both. But if you can fool her, if you can play her game and win, you'll be flown to the nearest city, Saint Petersburg, and released. It's your ticket out of this whole mess. Then you can do what they want you to—go to the authorities, tell your story. But of course, what they won't know is, you'll be telling the actual truth about everything. As for what happens then . . ." His father's distorted face was fading now. "I don't know. Either the good guys will win, or the bad guys will. But whichever side makes it . . . at least there'll be a you and a me. Someplace."

The message ended, and the image disappeared.

"Oh, Dad," Adam breathed. *Have you saved me—or is Josephs going to kill me right here?* Then he thought of Zoe lying crumpled on Keera's body, sleeping soundly while hungry creatures gathered around her. *I hope you didn't wake up. I hope you . . .*

Now the tears began to come. But with them came a pressure. Adam shook his head; a burning pain was building in his temples. Some side effect of tampering with the brainwash technique?

Wiping his nose, breathing deeply, Adam pressed his forehead against a panel of cold safety glass in the door. *You can do this. You'll be released, get back to Dad for real, warn everyone.*

Then he realized he could see an eerie green glow through the glass. There were four large glass tanks lined up like coffins in the middle of the room. *What the . . . ?*

He saw long red hair inside the nearest tank, like

Zoe's. It floated like some exotic seaweed, hiding whatever else was inside from view.

Adam tried the door handle. *Zoe could still be alive. Maybe Josephs needed her for some other experiment.* The door opened easily, and he entered a futuristic hospital room suffused with that soft, undersea shine. A huge silver vat loomed beside him, and he recognized it in a moment: *a bioregenerator—Geneflow's machine for regenerating cells, which helped create Zed at the start of all this.* Cables stretched from the vat to the tanks, feeding them with power and nutrients.

And with a dull chill, Adam saw there was a girl inside the glass, shrouded in white plastic and floating in the green-lit liquid. The hair was the same, but it wasn't Zoe—at least, not the way Adam had known her. She had two legs. Her neck was straight, her fingers even and regular. This Zoe had been cured, her disability discarded, her old body recycled like so much cheap packaging.

The clone was covered in scales, a glistening hybrid creature. The ridges and cracks in her reptilian skin made it hard to judge age, but Adam reckoned this Zoe was only nine or ten. Her form was still evolving to its new design.

At least she's not dead, Adam told himself. *She'll live on in a way. But . . . how can this ever be the Zoe I knew . . . ?*

Adam looked away, confused and upset. As he did so, he saw that the tank beside her held another reptile hybrid.

The world seemed to tilt sideways.

It was himself he saw bobbing in the flood of nutrients, himself as a young child. Adam crouched closer to see, his face reflected back at him over the clone's.

What have they done? He felt angry, violated, helpless as he pressed a hand against the tank. *No person should have the power to do this,* he thought. *No one should be able to choose how someone will look, or act, or be.*

The hybrid looked so peaceful lying in the tank. Adam supposed they would train this new him, repress his memories, start him over as a loyal and happy Geneflow follower. "But you're not one of them—you're still me," Adam hissed. "Whatever body they build for you, you're me, and don't you ever, ever forget that—"

The words dried on his tongue as the hybrid's eyes snapped open. They seemed to gaze at him through the chemical slime. Adam stared back into his own eyes. Was there any intelligence inside this growing shell, or was all that to be added? It was hard to recognize what reactions, if any, played on the reptilian features.

Adam leaned forward, close to the glass. "*Never* forget," he whispered.

Then the pain in his head came back, hot and sharp, driving him to stand. Adam turned his back on the nightmare experiments in the room and almost ran back to the tiny room he'd come from.

He wasn't a second too soon. Footsteps outside signaled someone was coming.

Oh, my God, oh, my God . . . Flustered, Adam lay back on the couch, tried to stop his eyelids from twitching, tried to clear his head. The fake memories actually helped in that regard—they stood out in his mind like patches of fresh paint on an old wall.

He heard the door open sharply, couldn't help but flinch at the sound. He acted groggy, like he was just coming round from a long sleep.

There was Josephs, a shock gun in one hand, a beaker of water in the other. "Hello, Adam." She passed him the drink. "Here. You've been unconscious for some time. The cloning process does leave the donors a little disoriented, as well as thirsty." Her dark eyes scrutinized him as a butcher would inspect meat. "I imagine your memories of your time here are a little . . . hazy?"

Adam eyed her gun and gulped at the water. *Here goes.* "I remember you introducing me to your Russian army friends," he sneered. "Remember how they bragged about the White House attack . . ." It was like his brain was running cutscenes in a video game, the parts that broke up the game play—you had no control over them, you could only watch.

We both know none of it's real, he thought. *But everything depends on her believing that* I *believe.*

"Well, well." Josephs watched him, poker-faced, as he finished outlining the sham events. "I'd say your memory seems just fine."

Does she know? Adam pushed on with the bluff. "I don't

remember anyone telling me why you've bred Z. dactyls as well as the raptors and rexes. Why bother? How come you've made them able to swim as well as fly?"

"I suppose you find that unnatural, and therefore 'wrong' in some way." Josephs shook her head. "It is *efficient.* Our pterosaurs' prime directive requires swiftness in the air *and* at sea—so we have given them both."

"Yeah, well . . . good for you." Adam felt suddenly dizzy. "What's a . . . prime directive?"

"A core instruction, more important than anything." Josephs tutted. "You know, Adam, I'm a little disappointed in you. You haven't even asked about poor Zoe."

Adam froze. *Of course. Dad wasn't meant to wake me; I shouldn't know what's happened to her.* "Where is she?" he mumbled.

"Sorry. You've missed your chance now." Josephs glanced from Adam to the inner door that led to the tanks; was it amusement in her look or something harder? His sight was blurring; he couldn't keep focus. "You look tired again, Adam. I do believe you're going back to sleep."

"No . . ." Adam let the beaker slip from his hand. "The water. You . . . drugged me?"

"Yet again." Josephs nodded. "But you won't be able to hold it against me." Her voice began to distort as the drug brought in darkness. "You're going a long way from here, Adam . . . and a good deal closer to the end of the world."

o o o

Adam's senses kicked in fitfully on his way out from the base. He smelled the sweat of the men holding him by his arms, felt the wintry blast of the Arctic on his face. Colored lights blurred around the airstrip, a dark stripe in the snow.

But are they taking me away to freedom, he thought feebly, *or to the vault for recycling?*

"Soon be over," a voice echoed in his ear.

And suddenly his face hit concrete with a wet smack. Adam tasted blood in his mouth, heard a terrifying roar overhead. "No," he moaned, turning onto his back, trying to open his eyes. In a blur of light, he saw teeth like huge ivory blades swinging down toward him, felt heavy footfalls jar around him. Something heavy dragged across Adam's chest, rolled him over. There was blood all over him, but he felt no pain. The roar came again, triumphant, exultant.

Then there was just silence.

Adam turned over again to find fat white flakes of snow spilling lazily from a sky like charcoal. *I'm still outside.* A floodlight was shining. It was too quiet. Dread prickled at his spine. *What happened to . . . ?*

A giant dinosaur loomed over him, bloody drool stringing from its jaws. Corded muscles twitched and flexed all over its dark, scarred bulk.

"Ad . . . am," breathed the creature.

"Zed?" He shook his head dizzily and saw the remains of a mangled guard on the asphalt beside a small passenger plane. *I never left the airstrip. The guards must've dropped me when* . . . "Oh, Zed!" Relief crashed through him as huge scaly hands scooped him up. "I thought you were dead."

"Fell far," Zed grunted. "Broke bones."

"Are you all right now?" Adam felt the drug in his bloodstream hauling him back to blackness, willed his eyes to stay open. "Zed, Josephs is in there. She's killed Zoe . . . and Keera. They've . . . We've got to . . ."

Zed said nothing, but tightened his hold on Adam just a little. The snow went on falling as Adam gave in to sleep at last.

18 IN THE FOREST

Adam woke to find night had swollen purple over a landscape of lakes and forests. He had no idea how long Zed had been flying. He felt chilled, hungry and thirsty, exhausted.

With nothing else to do, he brooded on all he had seen in Geneflow's base.

Josephs kills. She creates life. She can never die. She can change someone, body and mind, completely.

She and her Z. creatures are pushing the whole world into the war to end all wars.

And who has the world got to stick up for it?

Me and a talking dinosaur.

Even as the bitter thought passed through his mind,

he pressed his face harder against Zed's skin. *I thought I'd lost you. At least while you're here . . .*

Suddenly Zed's stealth powers activated; his hide became a mirror to the wilderness beneath them, and for a sickening moment, Adam thought he was going to fall. Then through the numbing gale, he heard a low drone of rotors. The sleek design of a helicopter revealed itself from the wash of gray cloud ahead. Adam swore. The world was on maximum alert, and Zed would be a prime target for any power . . .

The next instant, Zed dropped into a steep dive at sickening speed into a snowbound forest. Adam cried out, clinging feebly to the dinosaur's arms as Zed swung his bulk this way and that through the towering firs, smashing branches to matchwood, using the collisions to help him brake. Only when the terrible crashing had stopped and Zed's massive three-toed feet were stamping through snow and undergrowth did Adam breathe again, slowly and shakily.

"Where are we?" Adam watched as Zed bit at the snow, slaking his thirst.

"Help," Zed echoed softly. "She is near."

"She who?"

"She . . . like me." Zed looked at Adam. "And she like you."

"I don't know what you're talking about," Adam complained. He knew Zed didn't mean to talk in riddles but—

Suddenly he heard voices behind him, a language he couldn't place. Whirling around, he felt a stab of fear as two tall figures dressed head to foot in khaki pushed through the forest brush, electroshock weapons gripped in both hands. Both men shouted in a language Adam didn't recognize as they aimed their guns.

But they were just a fraction too slow. Zed whipped out his tail and struck the tree beside them. The splintered fir struck the soldiers like a giant's club, smashing them to the ground—and they stayed there, not moving. Shivering with cold, Adam felt gingerly for pulses in the men's necks and found them. "They're just knocked out."

"Had no smell," Zed rumbled.

"They must be wearing antistink." Adam's voice sounded strangely deadened by the gloomy pine acoustics. He searched the men's pockets, and in one he found a chocolate bar. Greedily, he tore open the wrapper and pushed the whole thing into his mouth, swallowing it almost whole. "You think these soldiers are from the Russian army?"

Zed snorted his ignorance.

Adam picked up one of the fallen shock weapons. "One thing's for sure, they must be out hunting for dinosaurs."

The black eyes fixed on him. "For *her.*"

"Her who?" Adam sighed. "Zed, if you can't smell the soldiers, we could walk straight into another attack."

"*Hear* them. Far off." Zed set off through the Christmas-scented forest.

Stomach aching with nerves and hunger, still holding the shock weapon, Adam followed him. The trek seemed to go on forever, and he found it hard to stop shivering. The drone of more copters wafting overhead unnerved him, adding to his fatigue.

Finally, the forest appeared to thin out. Adam noted more trees fallen than were standing. Some seemed to have been completely uprooted; others stood smashed and splintered at head height. It was as if a plummeting aircraft had come crashing through the firs, or . . .

Or a pterosaur.

Zed moved aside, turned to look at Adam with dark eyes. "Kee . . . ra."

How? For a long while, Adam was completely lost for words. He wasn't even sure it was really Keera; the beast was in a terrible state. Her skin was a glistening gray-white, save for three huge, festering gashes clawed into her side. One wing looked broken, rimmed with thick black crusts of blood. Her feet were mangled, half the talons wrenched away. Her blackened eyes were closed, and her enormous jaws sagged open as she panted for breath.

"No, she's dead." Adam looked away from the pathetic, half-broken animal and gripped his stolen shock gun. "This must be another Z. dactyl—they're clones, remember?"

At the sound of his voice, the creature stirred. Her eyes opened, and she tried to shift her weight, to turn toward him.

"Her." With a hiss and a snort, Zed turned, lowered his head closer to the ground and stomped away back into the forest.

"Zed, wait!" Adam called hoarsely. "Where are you—"

But the Z. rex had gone.

"How can you be Keera?" Adam whispered, a savage spite stealing into his voice. "Keera's dead."

A low, rasping chitter came from the creature as if in mournful reply, and she opened her jaws wider.

And Adam saw a muddy bundle stir inside. It was a girl, her face ghostly white. She smiled at him weakly, wonderingly, her matted hair as red as the bloody scratches on her cheek and neck.

This is impossible it can't be her it's a ghost no way this is crazy—

"Is this for real?" the girl whispered. "Adam?"

"Zoe!" Dropping the gun, Adam ran to the pterosaur's jaws and dragged Zoe free. "Zoe, is it—is it really you?" He saw the warped neck, her big fingers, and could've kissed them. "It's you."

"Of course it's me, you dumb pom!" She held him, but her grip was weak, and her skin and clothes were crusted with blood and dark brown mess. "Got any food?" She was shivering with cold. "Not eaten in days."

He felt a sudden flare of guilt for the chocolate bar

he'd just devoured. "I . . . no, I don't. I'm sorry. I'll find something." He laid her down, unzipped his Geneflow jacket and wrapped it around her. "I know it's not a sleeping bag—but it'll have to do."

Zoe took the warm coat gratefully. "It *does*." She licked the snow beside her, and Adam helped push some into her mouth. "Thank you. If this is a dream, don't wake me. I've felt so alone . . ."

"I saw you on security cameras," he told her, breathing through his mouth to shut out some of the smell. "How'd you ever get out of that place? I thought you were going to be eaten."

"I woke up to find jaws around me. But they were Keera's. She was trying to protect me." She closed her eyes. "I was so afraid . . . screaming. Trapped inside that cramped little space while Z. rexes kicked her and clawed and bit her and tried to open her jaws to get to me . . ."

Adam listened in horror; all he could think of was the scaly Zoe clone growing quietly in the tank while the real her suffered.

"Keera was too weak to fly, but she broke past them and squeezed into the pipe that took away all the dinosaur crap . . ." Zoe looked up at Adam. "They kept clawing at her, but she didn't give up. She forced her way into this sewer place underneath. Dragged herself through miles of stinking darkness—or it felt like miles. Thought we'd never find daylight."

"But you did?"

"The sewer came out halfway down a cliff. Keera's wing was bad, but she forced herself to fly." Zoe shivered again. "She wanted to bring me to safety. Me, the girl who understood. That's what she was thinking all the time, I know it."

Adam looked at Keera. *You're incredible.* She was watching them both with clouded eyes, her breathing still so shallow. *Hang in there,* he thought. *We've all got to hang in there.*

"Keera's lost so much blood, and her head's been hurting again, and she's not eaten . . ." Zoe's arm curled feebly around him; Adam saw the trail of tears on her cheeks. "When she landed so badly, I thought that was it. That we'd both starve to death and never see anyone ever again. So, to find you and Zed—"

"I thought I was hallucinating when I saw you too," Adam murmured. "After the way my head's been messed with . . ." He told her briefly about all he'd been through and his reunion with Zed—even about Zoe's scaly, two-legged twin in the tank.

"It's so sick, all of it. To think we left a whole different you and me back there, under Josephs's control." She shook her head, too exhausted to muster real anger. "And, my God, Adam, if Geneflow are serious about stirring up World War III . . ."

"We have to warn people what's happening, starting with Oldman and Marrs and our parents. And"—Adam sighed, leaned in against Zoe, huddling for warmth—

"we also have to dodge the soldiers out looking for you and Keera. They've got shock weapons."

"Soldiers from which army?"

"I don't know. But we've got Zed on our side. He's not fully healed, but he's still tough as hell. And I picked up a shock weapon."

"Don't mess, huh?" Zoe coughed weakly. "My hero."

"Get in line, lady!" Adam teased. "I'm here to save the world."

"I forgot that for a moment," Zoe admitted. He saw the resilience in her eyes as well as the pain.

Look at us, thought Adam. *No wonder Josephs wants to wipe out the likes of me and you. Weak and hurting and scared . . .*

And more determined now than ever to stop this madness—whatever it takes.

19 DAY OF DELIVERANCE

The shadows in the forest grew longer with the passing of the day. Adam and Zoe waited for Zed to return. Finally he arrived with several dead moose and reindeer crammed into his mouth. He spat the bodies on the floor in front of Keera. She gave a low moan and turned her jaws away from the offering. Zed growled a rebuke and kicked one of the carcasses closer. Reluctantly, Keera started to gnaw on its front legs.

"Kind of romantic, huh?" said Adam, a little queasily.

"They should get a room," joked Zoe through chattering teeth. "Do you think we should get some more snow, bathe her wounds again?"

"It looks like some of the cuts are closing up. We don't

want to reopen them." Adam looked at Keera worriedly. "Then again, what do I know?"

"At least she's eating something. That's got to help." Zoe shivered and hugged herself more closely. "God, I'm freezing. If we're out here when night falls . . ."

Adam nodded gloomily. "I know. We need to find help from somewhere. I just wish we knew where we were."

"Latitude, sixty-two-point-four," Zed barked, "longitude, twenty-nine-point—"

"He has GPS in his head," Adam explained to a startled Zoe. "Um, that's not much help, Zed . . ."

The monster crunched up a raw moose in three gut-churning bites, then straightened to his full, awesome height, his head nudging the treetops. "Soldiers come." He bared his teeth, started to flex his claws.

"No, Zed. You could get hurt if we fight—and we can't run and leave Keera defenseless. She needs help. And Zoe and I need shelter." Adam got up stiffly. "Maybe this time I should try to talk with the soldiers first. Hide out somewhere, okay? If things go badly, you can come steaming in. If they go okay, wait for me here. Keep out of sight. I'll come back for you." He crossed to Zed and looked up into the animal's narrowed eyes. "Whatever happens, it'll be all right," he murmured, "'cause if I get into real trouble, I know you've got my back . . . Haven't you?"

Zed stared down at him. The tip of his tail curled

round and brushed briefly against Adam's spine. Adam nodded. Then the Z. rex turned and stole away with an almost birdlike gait into the forest.

As the crack and clatter of his exit faded, Zoe looked nervously at Adam. "Wonder how long till they find us—"

Then the ragged curtain of the clearing seemed to burst open as men in fatigues pushed through the shattered undergrowth, some with shock weapons, others with assault rifles or grenades. Keera shifted, moaning softly as her eyes slid closed. One of the men started babbling in a high, excited voice, gesturing to Adam and Zoe with his gun.

"English!" Adam shouted, pushing his arms high in the air. "Don't shoot, please!"

The men's leader, pale and blond, spoke in stilted English. "Keep slow. Step away from this creature, please."

"No!" Zoe clutched Adam's stolen shock weapon and huddled closer to Keera's injured side. "Don't you dare hurt her!"

"We want to help her," the leader said calmly. "We are soldiers with the Finnish Army."

Adam blinked and felt unsteady. "Then . . . we're out of Russia?"

Zoe looked at him, triumphant. "Finland's part of Western Europe. We're okay!"

"I'm Adam Adlar," he told the soldiers. "This is Zoe—"

"Zoe Halsall. Yes, I had worked out as much." The man

smiled. "We didn't know if you would still be with the dactyl. Colonel Oldman will be very pleased."

"Oldman?" Zoe echoed, wide-eyed.

Adam couldn't believe it. "You've heard of him?"

"Right now he is my commanding officer," said the man wryly. "We're out here looking for this beast on his orders." He pulled out a walkie-talkie and started a conversation in his own language, which made as much sense to Adam as the squawks of static in between. "I just radioed for a chopper to airlift this animal."

Adam could hardly dare believe it. "Really?"

"Yes. Now we will take you back to camp."

"Can we trust them?" Zoe whispered. "It sounds too good to be true."

"I want to trust them," said Adam. "I'm too tired and cold *not* to trust them."

"Well, if we're going somewhere, I need a stretcher." Zoe giggled. "And a bath. And chocolate. Oh, and an artificial leg." She started to laugh. "Not necessarily in that order."

Adam started laughing too, letting out the tension, dizzy and hysterical. "We're all right, big guy," he yelled, hoping Zed would understand. "Wait for us, okay?"

The soldier looked puzzled. "Who do you speak to?"

"Er . . . just my invisible friend." Adam laughed until his ribs hurt, falling back in the snow, yelling thank-yous up at the sky.

o o o

The sheets were starched, and the bed was hard as a plank, but to Adam—after all he'd been through—the field hospital offered five-star luxury. And it was just a tiny part of Deployable Joint Command and Control, a mobile military base set up by Colonel Oldman thirty miles from the Russian border.

The hospital itself was basically a large tent full of medical equipment, warmed by electric radiators. The only other patient was Zoe, sleeping in the next bed to his own, clean now and smelling a whole lot better. When a young Asian medic in khaki came in with a plate of sausage and scrambled eggs, Adam thought his heart might burst.

"Hot food!" He shoved a whole sausage into his mouth in one go. "Mmm. Unbelievable."

The medic smiled. "Good, huh?"

"The best."

"I think I've got something you'll like even better." She gestured toward the tent's canvas doorway. "Mr. Adlar, he's ready to see you . . ."

"Huh?" Adam spilled egg down his shirt. "Dad's *here*?"

"Ad!" Mr. Adlar pushed inside and ran full tilt to his son's bedside for a tight, clumsy hug. "Oh, Ad, I've been so afraid."

"Me too," breathed Adam, gripping his dad right back.

"I never gave up hope. I prayed and prayed that you'd

be all right." Mr. Adlar looked up at the medic. "He is all right, isn't he? And Zoe?"

"They'll be fine," the medic agreed. "Gave us quite a scare when they were brought in—exhaustion, dehydration, early stages of hypothermia. But they got here in time. We just need to keep them under observation for a while."

"Under observation is right." Mr. Adlar's broad grin defied the weariness in his face. "I'm not letting him out of my sight." He gently disentangled himself from Adam and wiped a little egg from his shirt. "You know you've been gone for seven days."

"A whole week?"

"But it's okay now. We're together."

"Together . . ." For a second, Adam's sight blurred and he glimpsed *another* face on his father's body—one that was monstrous, reptilian. He shuddered, fell back on the pillow, blinked the image away. "Dad, it is you, isn't it? Really you?"

"Of course it's me." His dad smiled. "Ad, I must've called you a thousand times on your phone but couldn't get through."

"That's 'cause Geneflow hacked it." Adam stared at his dad, at the worry in his face, and felt a surge of self-pity for all he'd been through. "Dad, it's been so horrible. Josephs is alive—"

"Josephs?"

"She's a clone, and she's got a clone of you, and he tricked me into going to the Geneflow base." The words went on spilling from him in a torrent. "And they copied me and Zoe too, but they're changing everyone into reptile things, with tough bodies to survive this nuclear war they're going to start, and then—"

"Easy, easy, slow down." Mr. Adlar's frown deepened as he stroked his son's forehead. "Whatever happened out there, you're safe now."

"We're not, though." Adam let his head sink back into his pillow. "I've got so much to tell you. We've been with Zed! He's out there in the forest!"

"Zed?" Mr. Adlar's jaw dropped a little lower. "You're sure?"

"He saved me! See, I didn't escape from the Geneflow base with Zoe and Keera, I—"

"All right, Ad." Mr. Adlar placed a soothing hand on his shoulder. "Where is Zed now?"

"In the forest. Waiting for me."

"Well, no one's searching the woods now that Keera's been found. He ought to be safe there for now." Mr. Adlar put his head in his hands. "I think you'd better tell me just what's been happening."

So Adam went over his adventures in low, hushed tones. It felt so good to get it off his chest.

But by the time he'd finished, his dad looked pale. "I can't believe what you've been through. I'm so sorry, Ad. I wish I could've protected you."

"Well, it happened. At least now we've got a chance

to do something about it." Adam sighed. "How's Keera doing?"

"She's in a bad way, but she's right outside. Under the tarpaulin, being treated by Eve and a bunch of zoologists."

"Zoe's mum's here too?" Adam glanced at Zoe, but she was still asleep. "But, how did you know where Keera was?"

"Thanks to the circuits we found inserted in her brain." Mr. Adlar nodded. "The hangar was trashed after the battle to get Keera, but the computers recorded how you, she and Zoe communicated. The strength of her thoughts was off the scale."

"I know," Adam murmured, remembering Zoe's weird possession.

"And the reason it's so strong is because she's been fitted with a kind of neural transmitter."

"A what?"

"She can send out a powerful mental signal," his dad explained. "But as for *why* she needs to do that, we don't know."

"Something to do with her 'prime directive,' maybe," said Adam, remembering Josephs's words. "A core instruction, more important than anything else . . . which needs all the Z. dactyls they've made to be fast in the air *and* at sea . . ."

"All the security software loaded into their minds," Mr. Adlar mused. "Perhaps it's been placed there to protect this prime directive, in case of capture."

Adam slumped back on his pillow. "But what *is* it?"

Mr. Adlar shook his head. "Anyway, it was by tracing the signal on what was left of Eve's equipment that we knew Keera had reached Norway. But it was faint and intermittent. By the time Oldman had arranged aircraft to fly out of the mobile base, she'd moved on to northern Russia—where the signal died."

"Probably because she nearly died too," said Adam quietly.

"We couldn't very well follow in any case. The way things stand, a military expedition entering Russia's airspace would start World War III on the spot." Mr. Adlar sighed. "Those kidnapped scientists let loose from Geneflow has convinced a lot of important people that Russia is behind all this, that the country's ready for war. That's one reason why the Finnish government let Oldman set up base here, beside the Russian border."

"It's all just as Josephs has planned." Adam could've screamed with frustration. "We've got to make people see—she's trying to turn everyone against everyone else so we all wipe ourselves out!"

"Is this a classified conversation, or can anyone join in?"

Adam looked up, startled, to find Colonel Oldman had entered the canvas hospital. "Colonel, I'm so glad you're here."

"You have Keera to thank for that. Her signal has kicked in, on and off—that's how we knew to search the forests." A grim smile played around his handsome features. "I'm glad you and Zoe have showed up safe. But did I hear you say Russia is *not* responsible?"

"I was just telling Dad, Geneflow's setting them up," Adam told him, "making Russia seem like the bad guys."

Oldman looked unsure. "You'll have a tough time convincing General Winters otherwise. Those escaped experts are very credible witnesses. And after the attack in Mongolia this morning, half the politicians in the world are pointing fingers at the Russians and Chinese, saying they're in this together. Lots of angry denials and counter-accusations, of course. The Central Military Commission has taken control of the Chinese government—that means they're actively preparing for war."

"Josephs was planning that attack when I was brought to their base," Adam told him impatiently. "They were breeding new Z. rexes to make it happen."

"All right." Oldman was suddenly brisk and business-like. "Adam, I need everything you've learned from Geneflow, every last scrap of information. Your testimony will be circulated to Washington and the G8 powers for discussion moving forward."

"Adam needs to rest," Mr. Adlar protested. "He and Zoe are children, not soldiers—"

"Then read them a bedtime story when I'm through!" Oldman boomed. "I don't like this any more than you do, Bill, but the fact remains—we badly need intelligence on Geneflow, and whatever Adam knows, he needs to spill it." He turned to Adam. "You're looking a whole lot better already, Adam. Are you good for this?"

Adam looked uneasily up at him. "Do I have a choice?"

"Yes," said Mr. Adlar, steel in his eyes as he met Oldman's stare. "He does."

"Then . . . I choose yes." Adam sat up, his guts full of butterflies. "Let's go."

20 SHADOWS IN BLUE

Hours later, huddled in warm clothing, Adam left Oldman's command vehicle escorted by his dad and a bundle of armed soldiers. He'd told a bunch of army types everything he could recall of his time in the Geneflow base, raising several eyebrows and arguments in the process. His throat was sore, and he felt drained. But at least the truth was out there now. He'd done all he could—on that particular front, anyway.

Now it was time to talk with Keera. For what sounded like it might be the last time.

"Eve reports that no one on her team can get through to Keera, and she's weakening fast," Oldman had said. "If Adam's heard right and that prehistoric freak really *does* has a prime directive, we need to know what it is.

For all we know, Geneflow's sending more Z. rexes to kill her and to trample all over us."

Wish my *Z. rex was here.* Adam imagined him alone in the forest. He wasn't sure if Zed felt fear, or stress, or loneliness like the humans who'd made him. Adam's dad had decided to keep quiet about Zed's presence in front of Oldman for now. They couldn't be sure he wouldn't react to the Z. rex as a deadly threat—or try to harness him as a weapon.

The wind bit at Adam's body as he crossed the camp—a collection of military vehicles, huge metal containers and canvas tents in the churned-up snow. At the far end of the camp, beyond a small frozen lake, were two more canvas tents. A long stretch of tarpaulin bridged the two like an extra roof, hiding their purpose from anyone overhead.

"Keera's in there?" asked Adam.

His dad nodded as they trudged on through the snow. "I'm so proud of you, doing all this. You must be exhausted. But if you can just get past the last security barriers in Keera's head to find that prime directive . . ."

"What if I can't?" Adam murmured.

"If Zoe's right, and Keera sees you as the one who made her what she is—the one who can set her free—she'll want to help you. And after what she's been through with Zoe, that bond will be even stronger." He smiled encouragingly. "We can only hope she'll respond to the two of you."

No pressure, then, thought Adam.

The soldiers held back at the entrance to Keera's canvas cave and gestured their charges to go through.

Once inside, Adam's heart plummeted. Keera lay like a gigantic beached whale under foil blankets, surrounded by men and women in scrubs and surgical masks, banks of machinery and all kinds of scientific equipment. Her form looked bleached of color, almost translucent, like a giant grub.

Adam looked away—and saw Zoe was there already in a new wheelchair, her mum connecting a spaghetti of cables from the now-familiar bank of controls to her special headset. As he and his dad approached, Eve looked up, smiled and rushed to greet them, spilling coffee down herself.

"Oh, Adam," she said, grabbing him in a bear hug. "When I heard you and Zoe were all right, it was like a miracle."

"It sure was," Mr. Adlar agreed, going to fetch a Think-Send helmet and its various connectors. "A double miracle."

Adam waved at Zoe. "It's official—we're miraculous."

"Tell me something I don't know." Zoe looked sore and bruised but so much better already. "Have you been telling your story to Oldman?"

"Uh-huh. I expect it'll be your turn after this."

"Can't wait." She rolled the wheels of her chair closer to Keera, a sad look on her face.

Adam held still as his dad returned and fitted the Think-Send helmet on his head. He looked at the pterosaur's pale, sticky skin, the bruised slits of her eyes. "Keera's dying, isn't she?"

Eve looked at the floor.

"It's those misfiring circuits in Keera's brain." Mr. Adlar sounded frustrated. "She's desperate to think for herself, but the circuitry still wants her to obey her programming. And that battle's gone on in her head since her fit in Washington."

"I don't get you," said Adam.

"When Keera broke off from the White House attack and went after you, she demonstrated free will." Mr. Adlar started up the U-R software on the nearest computer. "That conflict with her programming basically blew a fuse in her head."

"She's tough as hell, bounced back from the initial trauma," Eve jumped in. "But the more she's done her own thing, the more the interface between mind and machine has been hurting her brain. Killing more and more cells."

Adam sighed. "Zoe said before it was like lights going off in Keera's head." He turned to Zoe for confirmation and saw that she had rolled right up to the pterosaur, reaching out to Keera's damaged wing.

"Zoe!" Eve jumped up. "Get back, love, we're not ready."

"*Keera's* ready!" Zoe snapped. "She knows . . . knows we want to talk."

Keera's eyes snapped open and fixed on Adam.

"I'm switching on Think-Send," Mr. Adlar said calmly. "Nonessential personnel, keep well back from Keera, please! Charlie, monitor life signs. Eve, are you ready to record this?"

"Ready." Eve jumped into her chair, flicked a line of switches. The other scientists retreated to the walls of the tent, watching in fascinated silence.

"Blue . . ." Zoe jumped in her seat, threw her head back. "It's like Keera's seeing nothing but blue."

"Brain activity increasing," someone called. Adam recognized the same white-coated man who'd hooked him up in the lab at Patuxent. "Heart rate steady."

"Thank you, Charlie." Eve stuffed half a sandwich into her mouth as the computer screen beside her filled with flecks of light and static. "Jeez, something's coming through already."

Mr. Adlar looked at Adam. "Ready to talk?"

"Ready." Adam felt a buzz in the back of his head. A fierce feeling of pins and needles started to radiate through his body as he met Keera's dark gaze.

"Here we go," Eve breathed as a deep blue permeated the flickering screen.

"Give me this," Zoe called, distantly. "Give me the sky. Freedom."

I can't yet, Adam told her in a thought. *There's still something in the way. Your prime directive—*

Zoe gasped, as if she were the one feeling pain. "Can't talk."

"It's like before," Eve fretted. "Keera's thoughts are filling Zoe's mind."

"The two of them are linked," Mr. Adlar agreed.

"Can't talk," Zoe said again.

"You can," said Adam, out loud.

"Can't. Metal in head."

"Heart rate increasing," Charlie called.

You are stronger than the metal in your head. Adam closed his eyes and concentrated. *Zoe and I are here. We'll help you.*

"Can't . . ."

You can. *You knew me from halfway across Washington because—*

"You fly through my thoughts," Zoe breathed. "From first day."

Right. Because you got more than just my brain waves when Geneflow trained you. You got a part of my spirit. He opened his eyes, glanced at the screen. Still static. *And so you should know that when someone tells you not to do something, it makes you want to do it even more.*

"Yes."

So tell me. Prime directive. He tried to shut out the rush and whir of his dad and Eve's equipment, the beeping of monitors, even the rustle of canvas in the icy wind. *Come on, Keera. If you can beat the metal in your head now, you'll beat it for good. You'll get strong again.*

"Wow." Charlie sounded tense. "Big spike in brain activity."

"Image changing—I'm getting something else," Eve hissed.

Adam looked. The screen was a mistier blue. A dark shape, tubular with stubby wings, was just visible.

What is that? asked Adam.

"Interference . . ." Zoe shook her head. "Frequency . . . jamming . . . all communications . . ."

"Her heart rate's going through the roof. I don't know how safe it is to continue—"

"We have to, Charlie." His dad sounded unhappy and strained. "What's she showing us, Ad?"

"The sea," Zoe said dreamily. "We're under the sea."

Adam saw the shadow on the screen grow larger, more substantial. A whale, maybe? A sea monster?

Think harder, Keera, he urged her. *Get Geneflow out of your head, and there'll just be me. Please, Keera, show us. Show* me.

"Think. Think to block it. Won't hear . . . won't receive . . ." Zoe was nodding. "Fail-safe. Fail-deadly. Fail-safe. Fail-deadly." She went on repeating herself.

"Zoe?" Eve sounded worried.

"Keera's life stats are off the graph," Charlie called.

Eve banged her fist on the desk. "We need to stop this."

"A few moments more," Mr. Adlar pleaded.

"That poor animal's mind is breaking down," Eve snapped, "and it could take Zoe's with it!"

The pterosaur began to jerk and twitch. The sinister, tubular shape loomed again on the screen. Dazzling yellow beams burst from inside it, and the screen flared like it was going to explode.

Then Keera threw open her jaws and screamed. Zoe cried out too as she was thrown backward out of her chair.

"No!" Eve shouted, and pulled a whole bunch of wires from the console. Sparks spat, and the screen went dead. While Mr. Adlar stabbed at switches, trying to power down safely, Adam yanked off his headset and ran with Eve to help Zoe, who lay on her back, arms spread wide like they were wings.

Keera was lying motionless save for the rapid rise and fall of her battered chest, her eyes closed, curled up in a heap.

"Vital signs settling," said Charlie. "It's okay. She's out of danger."

Eve was too busy checking over Zoe to comment. "Pupils dilating," she reported. "I think . . . Zoe? Sweetheart, can you hear me?"

"Mum?" Zoe smiled faintly, closed her eyes again. "We have the sky back."

"Excuse me?" said her mother.

Mr. Adlar came up behind Adam, put both hands on his shoulders and puffed out a sigh of relief. "You know, I think we just watched mind beating machine."

Adam nodded shakily. "But does it bring us any closer to beating Geneflow?"

21 ZEE NO EVIL

The camp's doctors had decreed that for Adam and Zoe there could be no more excitement till morning. Both needed bed rest, and that was what they were going to get. Even so, Zoe had refused to leave Keera's side for a couple more hours, until she was certain the pterosaur was okay. And Adam had lingered too, his head hot and buzzing with all the beast had left behind.

How long will it take Oldman and his experts to make sense of that stuff Keera shared? Adam remembered closing his eyes in the near-darkness, longing for sleep to come and soothe away the images. But it was broken sleep, so full of wearying dreams it made the night seem like a marathon.

Finally, grave male voices filtered through his senses.

". . . The apparent sighting of 'living weapons' in the skies over Iran has created fresh turmoil in international relations."

"Yes," a second voice agreed, "Israel has accused its Middle Eastern neighbors of attacking their parliament amid sensational claims that the Russian Federation has funded and supported these hostilities in association with the People's Republic of China—"

The voices clicked off. Adam opened his eyes to find Zoe's fingers at the off switch of a digital radio on the table beside her. The two of them were alone in the hospital tent. Thin daylight skulked at the edges of the canvas walls; the clock read five thirty A.M.

"Sorry," she said softly. "Didn't mean to wake you. How're you doing?"

"Better than the world is, by the sound of things." Adam pushed himself up in bed and winced. "Ow. Headache."

"Typical whinging pom," she said, mock annoyed. "Every news channel is full of experts telling us we've never been closer to global catastrophe, and you moan about a headache."

"I'm just a wuss, I guess," said Adam wryly. "How about you?"

"I'm okay, now that I know Keera is doing a whole lot better." Zoe smiled for real now. "Adam, can you believe it? We got through to her. Now that the Geneflow tech in her brain's been switched off, her cells will recover. Accelerated healing's already kicked in."

"It's amazing the way the Z. animals can do that . . ." Adam noticed the time and trailed off. "Hey, I just thought—poor Zed. He'll be out in the forest still; he's been waiting for more than a day."

"Well, he won't have to wait much longer." A figure stalked into the room, bundled up in a big trapper's hat, several scarves and a huge fur coat that made him look like a big fuzzy barrel.

Despite the disguise, Adam recognized him at once. "Dr. Marrs!" But his welcoming grin stiffened as he processed the doctor's words. "What do you mean, Zed won't have to wait much longer? How did you know he was near?"

"Where did you even spring from?" added Zoe.

Marrs waved away their questions. "Detestable cold," he grumbled. "I flew here direct from an emergency meeting of the United Nations Science and Ethics committee in sunny New York—although frankly, right now 'united nations' is a contradiction in terms." He mopped his furrowed brow with one of the scarves, as if suddenly finding it too warm. "Happily, the gathering I've just attended was more productive—an analysis of the information you freed from Keera's brain."

"What have you found out?" Adam asked. "If you're

here at five thirty, it must be something big. What's Zed got to do with it?"

"If I might get a word in edgewise, I'll explain." Dr. Marrs smiled. "I thought you'd be interested to learn the nature of that mysterious shadow thing in the blue."

Zoe sat up. "I thought it was just a whale or something."

"We believe it to be a nuclear submarine."

Adam and Zoe swapped dumbstruck looks.

"Do you remember what Keera said when she showed you that image?"

"Uh . . ." Zoe closed her eyes and her lips moved lightly as if whispering to herself. "'Interference,'" she said. "'Shouldn't receive. Fail-safe. Fail-deadly,' again and again. That was about it, wasn't it?"

Adam shrugged. "Sounds like gibberish."

"*Fail-deadly* is a term used in nuclear military strategy," said Marrs. "You may have heard of a fail-safe mechanism—a device that ensures that should a piece of technology or a system fail to perform correctly, no harm is caused to the user. Have you?"

"Nope," said Adam.

Marrs frowned. "Well, anyway, a fail-deadly device is quite the reverse. Should the system fail to perform, there will be automatic and overwhelming destructive consequences."

Zoe looked like she was trying to get her head around it. "Has this got something to do with nuclear war?"

"It has." Marrs looked grave. "A country's nuclear submarines must surface regularly to receive communication from their controllers. At a time when war seems imminent, they surface more often. In the event that no communications whatsoever are detected, the sub crews can only conclude that a nuclear attack has wiped out their homeland while they were out of contact beneath the sea."

"Oh, God," Zoe muttered. "And so those subs then retaliate by firing *their* nuclear missiles?"

"That's what I'd call an epic fail-deadly." Adam shook his head blankly. "But how does that fit with Keera's prime directive?"

"You know that the Z. dactyls can dive deep under the sea," said Marrs. "A nuclear sub could easily detect an enemy craft in local waters—but Keera and her kind would show up on radar as organic marine life, no threat at all—particularly as all attacks so far have come from the air."

"'Interference,' 'shouldn't receive' . . ." Zoe's voice had grown husky. "This neural transmitter thing in Keera's head—could it block a nuclear sub's communications?"

"It could indeed," said Marrs.

Adam grasped the implications. "So Keera's prime directive was to dive down and target a nuclear sub, then block its communications gear so no signals could get through."

Zoe nodded. "The captain thinks a nuclear war has

happened, when really it hasn't, and fires off a ton of missiles."

"Not realizing he's actually making a *first* strike," Marrs agreed. "Launching the first missiles that will drag every nuclear power into war."

"But, come on." Adam felt sick. "There must be special checks or something the subs can make to be sure they're not messing up?"

"Ordinarily, I'm sure," Marrs agreed. "But remember, after recent events, the likelihood of imminent nuclear war has never been higher. And who knows how many pterosaurs Geneflow possess? If they target fifty or one hundred nuclear subs, all it takes is for one of them to believe the worst has happened—"

"The sub's crew will fight back and start the war themselves." Adam remembered Josephs's words back in Russia: *tensions must continue to rise.* "Geneflow must be waiting for world relations to get even worse before they launch."

"But the attack could come any minute." Zoe stared at Marrs. "Can't we warn everyone?"

Marrs smiled patronizingly. "I can't see China and Russia standing down their nuclear weapons because we ask them nicely, can you?"

"Then how *are* you going to stop them?" said Adam.

"That's what we are trying to organize now," said Marrs gently. "And you do understand we must clutch at any chance to prevent this. Any chance at all."

Adam's eyes narrowed a touch. "Like going to Zed for help?"

"To your remarkable friend and a lot, lot further." Dr. Marrs tightened his scarf about his neck. "Perhaps you'd allow me to show you?"

Adam stood alone in the gloom of the Finnish forest. He stared up at the shaggy spikes of the tall firs all around and called out, trying to keep the shake from his voice. "Zed? Zed, can you hear me? I need to talk to you . . . need to ask you something."

There was no reply, no distant crunch of branches or beating of wings to signal the creature's imminent arrival. Just the low moan of the wind as it tugged down the temperature a few more degrees. Adam glanced behind him toward the armored truck he knew was parked just a few hundred yards away. Wondered if his dad and Dr. Marrs were still wrangling inside it as they had been all the journey from the camp.

"I can't believe you left the briefing early to coerce my son into doing this."

"I don't believe in patronizing the young, Bill. I needed to explain the situation as it was."

"You scared the hell out of him and Zoe. No kids should have to go through what they've experienced. They've been used by both sides—"

"If the situation weren't so desperate, I would naturally

accept your concerns. But the thought of what they will experience if we don't *do this . . .*"

Adam called out again, "It's all right, Zed. This isn't a trick or anything. The soldiers are only here to look after me and Dad. I need to ask you to work with them as well as us."

A fresh gust of wind rustled the branches and a dark green shimmer stained the air before Adam as Zed appeared. Taken by surprise, Adam backed away a few steps. Zed's tail snaked around behind him, its tip touching his spine.

"No soldiers," came the guttural growl.

"They promised me they won't hurt you," said Adam softly. "And I believe them. They need you. The whole world is in big trouble, and it's going to be game over, unless . . ." He couldn't really believe what he was saying; it sounded too fantastic. But he remembered Dr. Marrs's words: *How does the entire world come to find itself at the mercy of a small organization with no nuclear weapons of its own? In the main, because Geneflow has conjured the impossible from thin air—living weapons, a threat against which our traditional defenses are wholly inadequate. Our only chance is to fight fire with fire—turn their own creatures against them.*

Adam took a deep, shivering breath. "See . . . it's like this, Zed. The only way to stop Geneflow is to send in soldiers under the Russian radar and stop Josephs and her buddies for good. Stop them before they push the human race into a nuclear war—and then take whatever's left of the planet for themselves."

Zed stared down at him, breathing softly, black eyes cold and bright.

"I wish I didn't need to ask you," Adam rambled on, "but we could really use your help getting inside their underground city. See, you can go into stealth mode, sneak up on the base—Geneflow don't know that you're around. You'd be, like, the military's secret weapon to help them get inside." He looked up at Zed, searching out emotions in the colossal, scaly face.

He found none.

"Listen"—Adam tried another tack—"I know you hate humans. But you'd be getting back at Josephs, the one who hurt you. Who hurt *me.* Don't you want to get back at her . . . back at all of them? If we can't stop them, it's looking like the end of the world."

But even as he spoke, he knew that both times Zed had gone near a Geneflow base, he'd almost died—battling his own vicious clone the first time, torn half apart by Brutes the second.

It's me, Adam thought guiltily. *It's because of me he's been hurt so badly.*

"World ends." Zed pushed his shoulders up as if in a shrug and brought his face a little closer to Adam's. "We . . . fly away."

Adam half smiled, sadly. "Wish we could, Zed."

"Can." The brute head nodded. "Fly far."

"There's . . . there's nowhere far enough." Adam felt a faint prickle of tears at the back of his eyes. Zed was a miracle creature whose skills outshone those of troops and terrorists alike. He'd been trained with a thousand combat moves, he could defuse bombs and crack codes and commit countless acts of espionage. And yet while he knew so much, he understood so little. *It's like I'm the dad trying to break bad news to his kid in a way he'll understand,* thought Adam. *But* I'm *the kid.* Trying to talk his friend and guardian into what could well be a suicide mission, he found a part of him desperate to take Zed up on his deal—to run away and just give up. There would be someplace safe from the bombardment, wouldn't there? Some speck on the planet where life could carry on?

The desolation Adam had seen in the Geneflow simulation resurfaced in his mind. Suddenly he pictured the centuries-old forest and all its icy serenity exploding in the firestorm, the tall trees incinerated in a split second, nothing but ash shadows and scorched earth, poisoned and dead . . .

"Are you scared, Zed?" he murmured.

Zed looked past Adam toward the armored truck behind the trees, a growl building in his belly. Slowly, he nodded.

"Course you are. It was my brain waves that helped

shape you—and *I'm* scared to death." Adam placed a hand on the cracks and scales of Zed's gigantic tail. "I don't like trying to be brave. But I guess . . . some things you can't run from." Now it was his turn to shrug. "I don't want to go on this mission, and neither does Zoe, but we have to, yeah? Because we're the only ones who've been to the Geneflow base. And Colonel Oldman and his troops won't have time to scope out the place for themselves or set up weapons to try to break inside, 'cause once Josephs knows we're coming, she'll send everything she's got after us."

"Come." Zed moved his lips awkwardly, like he was chewing the words as he spoke them: "Have . . . to come."

"You're sure? You'll come with us to Geneflow's base?" Adam felt an uneasy mingling of hope, fear and guilt. "Thank you. Oldman's preparing the strike force at some old airstrip twenty miles from here. I have the coordinates written down . . ." He trailed off, unnerved by the intensity of Zed's stare. "Uh . . . you okay?"

"You." The word was a sandpapered whisper. "Got . . . my back?"

Adam swallowed hard and nodded. "Like you've got mine," he whispered. "Always."

The wind took the word and blew it into the conifer shadows. Then Zed flicked out his stubby wings.

"It's all right," Adam told him. "We're not due to leave till dawn tomorrow. There's last-minute stuff to test out or something." He forced a smile and pressed the paper into Zed's five-fingered hand. "Thank you. I'll . . . I'll see you first thing tomorrow. Come and meet me at the airstrip. Yeah?"

With a flick, Zed folded his wings away and nodded.

Adam turned and stumbled away toward the truck, his legs like water, his mind spinning. He could tell the grown-ups that he'd done it. He'd got the "good guys" their trump card, their surprise attack. But now he wasn't sure if he should feel proud of himself—or ashamed.

I just hope Oldman plays things straight, thought Adam. *And that setting up this mission isn't the last thing any of us will ever do.*

22 GOOD TO GO

"Won't be long now."

Adam stirred from his half sleep. The driver of the all-terrain vehicle was a big, dark bear of a man, and his voice drowned out its rumbling engines with ease. "The party should be happening just over the next hill."

A tremor of anticipation shook Adam properly awake. Zoe sat in the bucket seat beside him, quiet but alert. It was still dark outside through the window, and he checked his watch: close to six in the morning. The news feed at the base had been filled with reports of anti-American demonstrations in Moscow and Beijing. Neither side would rule out the use of nuclear weapons.

Faint streaks of light were stenciling the dark. Dawn was on the approach. *We've taken an hour to cover twenty miles,* Adam reflected. *Wonder how quickly Zed will tackle the journey.*

Wonder if he's as scared as I am right now.

Zoe yawned noisily. "Is it too late to change my mind and go back to the camp?"

"You heard what Oldman said." Adam thought back to when the colonel had dropped in on them late last night. "We've been to Geneflow's base. We're expected to show them the way inside."

"If his spy-satellite pix of the city hadn't been so rubbish, we could've marked the entrance on them," Zoe complained. "I don't see why it takes two of us. You've got to go anyway to look after Zed, but me . . . I feel like a hanger-on."

"If anything happens to me, you're the only one Zed will trust," Adam pointed out. "Anyway, just sitting around waiting's got to be as tough as taking part."

"Oh, sure. Easily." She looked at him. "Who d'you think you're kidding?"

He smiled. "Not even myself!"

They managed a laugh between them.

"Anyway, at least we'll be going by plane," said Adam. "Not 'beak class.'"

Zoe nodded. "I hope Keera will be all right on her own. Mum said she's getting stronger all the time, but . . ."

"She'll make a miracle recovery. You'll see." The transport rocked a little as it crested the hill, and Adam peered out the window, ready to get his first view of the airfield. “Well, *we’re* here.” He turned from the tinted windows, frowning. “But where’s everybody else?”

Adam had expected his first glimpse of the strike force to be like something out of a movie: awe-inspiring hardware, fighter jets and assault helicopters gleaming in the fire of an enormous red sun, low in the sky . . . dozens of troops, good to go in a heartbeat when the call to action came. The reality was as different as it was disappointing. A thin mist hung like a ghostly veil in the air, partly obscuring the long, wide airstrip. There were trucks and transporters and tankers and ground crew, but—

“No planes?” Zoe frowned and turned to their driver. “What’s going on?”

“Wait a minute . . .” As the car rumbled on down the slope toward the military ants’ nest, Adam thought he could see sharp lines and graceful steel curves mingled in with the mist. “Am I seeing things or—”

“Not *supposed* to be seeing things,” said Zoe, wide-eyed. “OMG, Ad. They’ve got stealth tech going on down there!”

It was like some Magic Eye puzzle scattered over real life; Adam could just discern the bulk of a passenger aircraft through the haze. He soon found the trick was not to look at it directly but to observe from the corner of his sight. “They’ve been studying Keera for almost a fortnight,” he murmured. “Makes sense they’d want to know how she turns invisible.” He narrowed his eyes;

farther down the strip, he could just make out two more planes, massive, heavy-duty constructions.

Air transporters, he realized. *One of them must be there to carry Zed.*

"This has got to help our chances, right?" Excitement was shining now in Zoe's eyes. "I can't believe they didn't tell us they'd done this!"

"It makes sense of why they're willing to risk crossing the Russian border," said Adam more cautiously. "I heard at the Pentagon that the Z. beasts slipped past radar systems in stealth mode, so if we can do the same . . ." He looked up and saw a hazy shape circling high above in the lightening sky. "Oh, man. Heads up."

"Zed?" Zoe peered up through the window. "Wow. We really *are* using Geneflow's own weapons against them."

As their armored transport got closer, Adam could hear a fierce, protesting drone, like generators being run to their limits and beyond. Finally it wound down, like a screaming mechanical siren, and as it did so, the plane and the air carrier began to shimmer into plain sight.

"Your escorts will take you from here," called the driver, hitting the brakes as three soldiers ran briskly up to the vehicle. He pointed to the big white jet adorned with stripes of pale blue. "And you'll be riding in style. That's a VC-25A, military version of a Boeing 747. Worth three hundred and thirty million dollars. The president's own plane."

Adam swapped a nervous glance with Zoe. "Wow."

"Those other two are C17 Globemaster IIIs," the driver went on conversationally. "Heavy lifters. They can air-drop over a hundred paratroopers with equipment."

Or one dinosaur, thought Adam. Then the doors of the vehicle were yanked open and stony faces were pressing in, arms extended to help him and Zoe down onto the tarmac. The cold air was intense, like a physical attack on the senses. "My friend needs her wheelchair," Adam began, his voice coming in puffs of steam. "It's in the back—"

"Copy that," came a familiar voice as someone appeared from the rear of the transport, wheeling the chair. "Welcome to the weirdest damn airport I've ever been to."

"Colonel Oldman!" Adam was taken aback; how many commanding officers took the role of porter?

It was Zoe who supplied the likely explanation: "How guilty is *he* feeling, dragging kids into this?" she muttered.

Oldman was out of uniform, dressed casually in jeans and a parka. "Glad you two could make it," he said as the soldiers helped Zoe into her chair. "Get the girl on board." As the two soldiers saluted and got to it, he turned to Adam. "Now we're waiting for your buddy Zed. You're sure that he'll—"

"He's coming, sir." Adam looked up at the blur in the

breaking blue above. It was growing bigger, a hazy streak on reality, descending fast. "He doesn't like soldiers. Please don't panic him or—"

"My crew has been briefed." Oldman spoke in a clipped tone. "You're here because you can handle him. I hope." He shook his head. "When the Special Activities Division brought me in to handle high-threat military operations, I never imagined . . ."

His words were lost in the thunder of Zed's arrival. The ground shook as two huge, three-toed footprints appeared in the tarmac and the force behind them grew visible—the dark, colossal bulk of the Z. rex, blotting out the newfound light. Opening his tooth-crammed jaws, Zed threw back his head and roared. Oldman fell back in alarm against the armored transport, but Adam stood his ground.

"It's all right, Zed!" he called up quickly. "No one wants to hurt you."

"That's right." Oldman recovered himself hastily, tried to act unbothered. "Uh, the report said . . . he talks?"

Zed suddenly pushed his massive head down and forward until it was level with Oldman's; the colonel held very still. "Here . . . for Adam." The words rattled from the monstrous throat. "Just Adam."

Oldman managed a single nod. Zed reached past him with a chunky arm and pressed his hand against the side of the all-terrain vehicle. Then he scraped his claws downward, a slow, nails-on-chalkboard effect, scoring the armored metal and bulletproof glass.

"Adam," said Oldman quietly. "Can you ask Zed to step into the back of this C17? We put some, uh, food in there . . ." He raised a hand toward the big plane, which had a massive ramp hanging down from the rear of its fuselage. A squad of soldiers was flanking the plane but keeping a wise and healthy distance.

"It's okay, Zed," Adam told him. "They're going to carry you so you can save your strength. I'll check the place out with you."

He crossed to the C17, Zed padding alongside him, tossing barks and growls at the soldiers around the airfield. The cargo hold looked a reasonable size—lengthwise it was longer than a train car, but about three yards high and three yards wide. Several hunks of meat had been piled inside. Zed looked at Adam for a few moments. Then he ducked his head and stepped lightly up the ramp, curling round like a dog finding a comfortable spot to lie down. He sniffed the food but did not eat—then looked at Adam, perhaps a little resentfully. Feeling sad, Adam mouthed a thank-you to him.

Oldman came up behind him. "We've fixed two-way coms so you'll be able to talk to him from our own plane when you need to—and he can, uh, talk to you." A pause, then he lowered his voice. "You're certain this . . . creature will do as you tell him?"

"As sure as I can be." Adam wasn't bragging; the admission made him feel bad. He raised his voice. "Zed, these people here are all my friends. Will you help them like you've helped me and do as they ask?"

The huge reptile shifted his head to one side and gave a soft, sulky snort.

"Think that's a yes," Adam murmured. *At least I hope so.*

Oldman hit a red button built into the fuselage. The ramp cranked slowly upward, sealing the bulkhead. Adam watched, heart pounding, as Zed was taken from his sight.

As Oldman strode off toward the VC-25A, which was humming and hissing while its systems came alive, he looked to be in a daze. "No wonder the government's gonna deny all knowledge if we blow this thing. Who the hell would ever believe them?"

Adam tagged along behind him. "What's the other C17 carrying?"

"Operatives from Delta Force, Navy SEALs, SAS Mountain Troop . . . the cream of NATO's special operations forces." Oldman nodded distantly. "Out of uniform, of course, and no ID, so they can't be traced—while their equipment was purchased from a private arms dealer."

"But if this is the president's air transport, isn't it going to be obvious—"

"Don't worry about the cover story. The Special Operations Group deals with this stuff all the time." Oldman looked up at the bare, blue and white expanse of the plane's nose cone. "It's already the most advanced aircraft on the planet. That's why it was fitted first with the super-stealth technology we adapted from Keera's cellular design. That might *just* get us past the Russian fighter jets patrolling the borders without starting a major diplomatic incident." He walked up the airstair to the plane's main entrance. "Come on. We're all aboard and good to go."

We are? thought Adam, his legs wobbling as he followed the colonel. The mist was thinning and the sky brightening over the surrounding moorland and the distant trees. But Adam felt a dark foreboding swell inside, and as he reached the door, he hesitated.

We've got one chance at this. Just one.

Will we make it back?

He looked toward the C17 and thought of Zed trapped inside . . . thought of Keera lying so sick and still back at the camp . . . thought of all the days he'd woken feeling sick and small and helpless. Thought of Zoe too, and his dad and Eve, of the carefree days they'd lost, forced down into danger.

One way or another, he thought, *that changes after today.*

Adam stepped inside, and the door swung shut on the cold blue sky behind him.

Adam was shown to a high-tech conference room on the top deck of the three-level plane. With the wood paneling, huge oak table and giant TV screen, it looked to be modeled on the Pentagon office he'd visited; only the many porthole-style windows studding the walls, their shutters half raised to let in the morning light, reminded him that this was an aircraft.

Zoe was already there, strapped into a leather seat, big fingers drumming on her jeans where her leg should be, watching her mum and Adam's dad at work. They were standing behind their untidy tumble of hardware and monitors, grappling as ever with multicolored cables. Only this time, the Think-Send headset had extra bits and bobs attached and was linked to a large metal box.

"Ad!" His father saw him, discarded a set of cables and scooped him up in his arms like he hadn't seen him in weeks. "I'm so glad to see you. Zed's on board the carrier safely? You're all set?"

Adam hugged him back but barely heard the questions and mumbled vague replies. The weighty realization filled his chest like cold water: *This could be the last day of all our lives.* But there was a sense of excitement fizzing among those fears. *Or maybe it could be the greatest.* He'd lived through so much, clawed his way through the craziest odds.

Just imagine if we actually made it . . .

A steady rush of turbines began to build, as though the airplane was gathering strength to fly. Adam felt his stomach twist with nerves—and then a dour-looking man appeared at the door. "Would you all get into your seats, please? We'll be taking off shortly."

"Who's he?" wondered Zoe as the man stalked away.

"Secret Service," Eve explained through a mouthful of croissant, spitting pastry flakes as she connected the last cables to a slew of wires protruding from a hole punched into the onboard comm console. "There's a couple of nice men with guns on board to keep us in line—doubling up as flight crew."

Adam looked at the lash-up. "So, what does that thing actually do?"

"Hopefully, and at its most basic, it's a dinosaur-jamming device." Mr. Adlar pressed a couple of buttons and looked relieved to find a number of red lights dotted around the construction glow into life. Then he patted the Think-Send helmet. “We’ll transmit a loop of random code; hopefully, that will be picked up by the Z. beasts’ brain implants and scramble their minds.”

Zoe nodded. “So they can’t be used as weapons.”

“Exactly.” Mr. Adlar crossed to the communications console and flicked a switch. “We’re up and running, Colonel.”

“Pleased to hear it, Bill,” came Oldman’s crackling reply. “Will your jamming device work?”

“We hope so,” said Eve. “There’s been no way to test it properly.”

“I think you’ll get your chance,” drawled Oldman. “You can bet Geneflow will send every dinosaur in the place to attack the moment they see us coming. Out.”

The speaker went dead.

Adam slumped down on the leather couch that ran the length of the cabin. “This thing won’t hurt Zed, will it?”

“Only slave animals given orders by Think-Send will be affected,” his dad assured him. “We just don’t know how *much* they’ll be affected.”

“Oldman wants those poor creatures alive if possible.” Eve fastened her seat belt with a loud click. “They’ll be key evidence in proving to the world that Geneflow were behind all this madness, not Washington or the NATO powers or anyone else.”

"Glad we've got stealth mode," said Adam. "Imagine if we were shot down before we even got close—"

"Could happen," said Eve gloomily, helping Mr. Adlar as he fumbled with his seat belt. "To simulate what Z. beasts do naturally takes an awful lot of power for a plane this size. Oldman's not certain how long the systems will stay operational . . ." She trailed off as she finally noticed Mr. Adlar's frantic mouthings to stop. "Uh, but it'll be fine. We don't have to worry, really."

Zoe rolled her eyes. "Great pep talk, Mum."

"So, just in case we *do* get there," Adam ventured, "do we know what happens then?"

Adam's dad nodded. "Oldman takes us in a flyby over Geneflow's ghost town so we can switch on the mind jammer—and you can get Zed to sniff out the entrance. Geneflow will no doubt attack him, revealing the way into their base in the process—and that's when Oldman deploys the special ops boys from the other Hercules, who'll parachute in with all guns blazing."

"Meanwhile, we'll have landed on that airstrip you talked about," Eve added. "Once the operatives have 'subdued' the resistance and secured the place, we go inside as expert witnesses and let Oldman know what Geneflow has been up to."

Suddenly the plane started to taxi forward. A chime sounded in the room. "As you might've guessed," came Oldman's voice, "we're taking off. We have a little over six hundred fifty miles to cover, and our flight time is estimated at seventy-five minutes. Out."

"Pilot's not very friendly," Zoe said. "I'm not flying this airline again."

Adam couldn't muster a smile. The whining rush of engines started to build and build, and then the push forward began in earnest. He clutched his armrests as the craft juddered over the airstrip, picking up speed.

Then the plane was angling upward, leaving the ground. Adam closed his eyes, trying to swallow his heart back down as it rose steadily up his throat. Within seconds, the plane was soaring through the watery clouds that streaked the sky. The airfield already a crazy distance below, the two Hercules-like model planes, one of them gliding forward now, signaled by men the size of mites in high-vis jackets, fluorescent specks against the asphalt.

A harder, more nasal whine stole into the air now—the same hum Adam had heard on the airstrip. As he peered out to his left, he saw the wing of the VC-25A fizzle and blur until it had vanished altogether. The body of the plane dissolved too, till Adam found himself looking at a haze of cloud and shadow.

"Wow," he breathed. "That is *awesome.*"

"Close the shutters on your windows, please." Oldman's voice over the speakers made him jump. "Leave them closed at all times. It's imperative we give no indication of our presence in Russian airspace. Electronic countermeasures are in force, and radio silence will be maintained. Out."

"Here we go," Zoe murmured.

Adam nodded. "Remind me to breathe again once we've crossed the border."

The aircraft crossed into Russian airspace without incident—aside from the commotion in Adam's guts as the tension took its toll—and the journey passed in slow, heavy silence. The hum of the stealth screen sent reverberations through the whole plane that made Adam's already sore head ache harder.

Often on planes, he liked to study the sky map showing their position in the air relative to cities far below. This particular aircraft offered an interesting twist—the TV on the wall showed the real-time view outside the plane as relayed by special cameras in the hull. The screen was split into four, showing the way ahead, the way they'd come and all that could be seen to port and starboard. A bleary shimmer on either side signaled the reassuring presence of the two C17 Globemasters, flanking the VC-25A in close formation.

"That's an hour we've been flying," Eve announced. "So far, so good."

Mr. Adlar nodded. "Another fifteen minutes till we reach the vicinity of the Geneflow base."

"We can do the math, Dad," said Adam quietly.

His dad ignored him. "We'd better warm up the equipment, Eve. Best to be ready."

Zoe groaned, her hands clamped over her stomach. "This is like torture."

Adam nodded. While Eve and Mr. Adlar started switching on their ramshackle rig, Adam's eyes stayed glued to the shimmers on the screen, praying the planes would remain hidden. Every muscle in his stomach felt ready to snap, his shoulders ached, and his neck clicked every time he turned his head.

Then he saw it. A dark blur on the screen to the rear of the plane. A mark on the lens? No. It was growing bigger.

Adam pointed, his mouth suddenly desert dry. "What's that?"

Zoe had seen it too. "It's a Z. rex!" she shouted. "Switch that thing on!"

Eve stared at the screen. "It's coming right for us!"

The plane banked sharply starboard. Zoe was strapped in, but Adam had undone his seat belt and found himself thrown across the conference room, slamming into the table. As the drone of the engines rose like a mechanical groan, Eve and Mr. Adlar struggled to stay standing, tweaking and turning dials and settings on their machine. The rearview image on the TV had shifted as they'd turned, showed nothing but cloud. But within seconds, the dark blur returned, larger now. And another speck was catching up behind it. Dragging his eyes away, Adam saw more specks rising up through the wisps of cloud.

"Geneflow's on to us." Oldman's voice sparked from

the speakers, rising over the urgent roar of the engines. "Z. beasts incoming. Bill, Eve, we need that jamming device."

An electronic grinding noise started up from the mishmash of electronics. Mr. Adlar hurled himself at the comm console and hit the intercom. "Signal transmitting," he yelled.

"They're still coming!" Zoe reported.

She was right: the hideous, bloated figure of a Z. rex was forming out of the clouds, jaws hanging wide, hurtling toward the rear of the plane. "It's not working. Why isn't it working?"

"That thing can't be in range," Eve shouted.

The plane dipped sharply, and Adam nearly hurled. "What was that?"

"Pilot must be trying to lose the Z. rex," Mr. Adlar guessed.

Zoe pointed at the screen. "He's steering us into *that* one!"

Another Z. rex, identical to the other in every terrifying way, was on a collision course with the cockpit. There was an almighty, booming clang as the monster impacted. The plane lurched so hard that only Zoe, still strapped in, didn't kiss the carpet. Adam looked up from the floor, saw that a quarter of the screen was now darkness and scales.

That Z. rex will tear its way inside in seconds, he thought grimly. *It's game over!*

24 MEETING OF MINDS

Adam stared at the screen in numb terror, expecting to hear the Z. rex tearing through the hull at any moment. But suddenly, the view of the sky cleared and the creature fell away, its limbs twitching, the jaws snapping open and shut uncontrollably.

"The signal's taken effect!" Mr. Adlar shouted, scrambling up to check the monitors. "Finally . . ."

"It took so long to go to work." Eve was frantically flicking switches. "I'll try to boost the signal."

"Don't!" Mr. Adlar grabbed her wrist and pulled her away. "If we blow the transmitter, we'll have no signal whatsoever!"

Adam was still staring at the TV screen. At the rear of the plane, a pterosaur just like Keera was drawing horribly close. At the last moment, it veered away, wings stiffening as it tumbled from view.

"But if it only works when those things are practically on top of us . . ." Eve's protest trailed away as she stared at the awful images streaming live across the TV.

"Oh, no," Adam breathed. With the 747 causing headaches, the C17s had become the beasts' prime targets. The carriers' gray exteriors flickered in and out of sight as the untried stealth tech faltered under the power of the prehistoric onslaught.

"What about Zed?" Adam's finger stabbed at the starboard carrier. "He's alone in there. If those things get inside—"

"At least he stands a chance," Zoe countered breathlessly. "What about the soldiers in *that* plane?" Against orders, she'd opened the shutter on her window, and Adam staggered across to join her. He bit his lip, feeling sick as he saw Z. rexes and pterosaurs cluster over the cockpit, clawing at the hull, hammering tails and beaks against its battle-scarred bulk.

"Oldman," Mr. Adlar, white-faced, shouted into the intercom, "we need to get closer to the C17s. If we can only clear them of Z. beasts long enough for us all to land and get those men out—"

"If we get that close, we risk a collision that could take us all out!" Oldman shouted back.

The swarm of creatures continued their ceaseless assault, mauling metal housings, wrenching at the wings.

Adam looked over at the screen, saw the other Hercules was under heavy attack too. "We've got to let Zed out of there!"

"Colonel Oldman." Mr. Adlar tried to speak calmly into the intercom. "Release Zed—he'll be more of a threat to the creatures like him. He might become their priority . . ."

"Buying time for my men to escape," Oldman agreed. "I'll warn the pilot to open the launch doors. Adam, I'll patch you through to Zed—give him the order."

Adam froze. He'd wanted Zed free to escape, not to become the prime target.

"Do it, Ad!" his dad cried. "Give the order!"

"Look!" shrieked Zoe.

Working together, two Z. rexes had managed to rip open the cargo ramp at the rear of the special ops carrier, the metal tearing like tinfoil. Soldiers spewed out from inside, free-falling in the arctic air. Some blasted bullets from assault rifles, others fired arcs of crackling yellow from electroshock weapons. One of the Z. rexes flailed in the blaze and lost its grip on the stricken Hercules, and as it fell, for a second Adam thought the men might stand a chance. But then the Z. dactyls appeared, dark jaws widening, snatching the soldiers from the sky even as they went on firing.

"It's a massacre," Zoe whispered.

Mr. Adlar was back at the intercom. "Zed? Can you hear me, this is Bill Adlar—"

"No. I'll do it." Shaking and nauseous, Adam pushed himself away from the window and over to the intercom. "Zed . . . you've got to come out. People are dying, so many people—Zed, if you can stop it, please . . . ?"

He looked up at the screen. One of the monsters was tearing at the loading ramp at the back of Zed's Hercules when it swung open—and Zed launched out from inside, teeth bared, claws already swiping at the nearest Z. rex. Only now that they were side by side could Adam see how much smaller and leaner Zed was compared to this new generation. The sludge-colored giant met Zed head-on, biting at his neck with savage ferocity. But Zed squirmed free, spun around and clubbed his opponent around the head with his tail, a blow so hard it sent the Z. rex tumbling into empty space.

"Bill, we've got to boost this jammer somehow." Eve was staring helplessly at the mass of wires as Mr. Adlar crossed to join her. "If we can't, none of us will stand a chance."

Adam watched, heart in mouth, as Zed launched himself into the monster feeding frenzy. He landed both clawed feet on the back of a pterosaur, gripped tight, then spun forward in a loop-the-loop, releasing his catch as he did so like a living, scaly shot put to take out the nearest two Z. rexes.

"Hurry, Dad," cried Adam.

Zed landed on top of the Hercules's starboard wing, and the giant aircraft rocked as four of his lethal relatives set about him. He dealt one Z. rex a blow that tore red from its throat before dispatching another with a flurry of kicks and body blows.

Come on, Zed. Adam rooted for him in silence, every muscle clenched.

"He's doing it!" Zoe was pulling at her red curls, rubbing them against her neck, rapt and breathless. "He's not as strong, but he's faster."

It was true: nimbler, more agile, Zed was able to dart in with his claws and then dodge out of range of the Z. rexes' counterattack. Blood stained the wings of the carrier aircraft. But then a pair of pterosaurs joined the battle. Each grabbed one of Zed's wings and twisted hard in different directions. Zed screamed out with pain and rage, a hideous keening that rose above the urgent rush of engines and the stealth generator's nasal whine. He wrapped his tail around the neck of one Z. dactyl and twisted hard, breaking its grip. Wings flailing, the pterosaur sailed straight into the Hercules's propellers and exploded into grisly chunks.

"Dad!" Adam shouted, tearing himself away from the gruesome scene. "Why can't you *do* something?"

Mr. Adlar looked up at Adam. "There's nothing we can do. But maybe . . . *you* can."

Adam frowned. "What are you talking about?"

"The trace of your brain waves in the Think-Send system." His dad looked to be thinking aloud. "We know you can boost U-R code just by concentrating—if we can plug your mind into the system here . . ."

Eve nodded. "It might boost the jamming signal."

"But it could be dangerous." Mr. Adlar held up the Think-Send headset, but looked conflicted. "This isn't a game program, Ad—it's random code, meant to completely disorient those creatures."

"I know," Adam said impatiently, "but I'm not a slave animal. I have free will, like Zed. It won't affect me—"

"Not in the way it will affect them, no. But don't you see? Your brain has to receive the signal before it can boost it, and this signal was never meant to mix with a human mind. It"—Mr. Adlar swallowed hard—"it could drive you insane."

Adam hesitated, suddenly scared.

"Quickly," groaned Zoe, staring out the window. "They're tearing him apart!"

"Zed thinks I've got his back." Almost without thinking, Adam snatched the headset and placed it firmly in position. "I've got to at least try."

And if I go mad, at least I'll never feel the teeth sinking in when they catch us.

Eve was already switching connectors, her hair plastered to her forehead with sweat. "Good luck, Ad. God help us, here we go."

Adam heard his dad voice last-moment doubts, but Eve hit the switch, and—

The real world vanished.

Like a leaf snatched by a hurricane, Adam was swept

into a screaming, wailing nothingness. Flashes of sound and light sliced into his senses. He couldn't think, couldn't feel. He was lost in a void of dark static that threatened to tear him apart.

This is the raw code, he realized dimly, *the building blocks of an Ultra-Reality program. This is what's being fed into the heads of those monsters out there.*

With excruciating effort, Adam tried to concentrate on the wild nothingness in his brain, tried to reach out and direct it. But it was no good; he was being swamped, and the pain was enough to—

<Oh, man, great minds think alike.>

Adam felt a jolt slam through his whole body at the sound of the voice. His *own* voice.

I'm going mad. Adam's sight was all black smears and static, but he could sense another presence in the maelstrom. *Someone else using Think-Send on my frequency, using my voice . . . ?*

<I can't believe you're in here with me! Your Think-Send, my Think-Send—we've connected and it's, like, multiplayer!>

Multiplayer? Adam's head was still spinning.

<Well, kind of. What was it you told me in the tank? "You're still me"?>

And suddenly, Adam could sense his mirror image close by, the features of his face distorted by green reptilian ridges. *It's you—I mean, it's* me. *The clone of me.*

<*Two of us—wouldn't that freak out the teachers back home?*>

The voice, slurring slightly, seemed to come from everywhere. *Speaking through Think-Send—this must be how Keera heard me talking.*

<*Right.*>

But how can you be in this Think-Send system?

<*Same brain waves, remember? I'm Think-Sending here at Geneflow's base; you're Think-Sending out there somewhere—it's like a wireless connection. Dad's got me trying to take control of the Z. beasts.*>

To use them against us?

<*To stop Geneflow for good . . .*>

The voice grew suddenly fainter, snatched away by the digital storm. Adam struggled to hold on to it. *You want to help us? But . . . Geneflow made you.*

<*Yeah, and look* what *they made me. They tried to change how I think too, but you know what? I thought of Zed. I thought of all they did to hurt him, to try and kill him. I guess because I* am *still you.*>

Zed's out there now. He's fighting, but he can't win.

<*I know. That's why I'm here, and we've got to be fast, 'cause pretty soon—*>

What? There was silence. Adam feared he'd lost his one point of contact in the chaos, felt panic start to rise. *Are you there?*

<*Listen!*> His own voice barked back at him from the

darkness. *<I'm trying to control the Z. beasts, but they're at the limit of the Think-Send's range.>*

I'm trying to boost the range of the Think-Send here.

<Maybe we can boost each other. If we think of just one command. One simple command—>

One simple command to deal with all those monsters? How can we . . .

Then the answer came to both voices at once: *stop flying.*

<They'll fall and crash-land—>

From, like, twenty thousand feet. Game over!

<So come on. Stop flying . . . Stop flying . . .>

Stop flying. Taking strength from the voice in his head, Adam spoke the words over and over, willing the simple command to bring structure to this virtual world of storm and static. He pictured the gnarled wings of Z. rexes slowing and stiffening, imagined pterosaurs, freezing in midair—and then falling . . . falling . . .

<It's working! Keep going. I . . . I can't help us any longer . . .>

What is it? Adam felt suddenly frightened. *What's happened?*

<You happened. You made Dad see what he'd become. Made him decide what he had to do about that . . .>

The voice was rising, getting really upset.

What? I don't get it.

<Just make sure you have the best life. The best life ever, for both of us, okay?>

The voice stopped, bringing a sudden emptiness to Adam's head. Confused and afraid, all he could do was keep his focus on that one command: *Stop flying, stop flying . . .*

Like a CD skipping, his thoughts stammered suddenly—*stopfly stopfly stopfly stop—*

And he was out of the darkness, wide awake, sweating and sprawled on the conference room floor, his weird encounter with himself fading in his mind like a dream. *Did any of that even happen?* His dad was holding the headset, staring down anxiously. Eve was on the couch beside Zoe, squeezing her hand.

Automatically, Adam looked at the screen. He saw a pterosaur tumbling out of the sky, wings rigid, and a Z. rex claw uselessly at the air as it plunged toward the icy wastes.

"It worked," Adam breathed.

"Yes, they were the last." Mr. Adlar nodded slowly. "Incredible. You stopped the Z. beasts, Ad. You literally knocked them out of the sky."

Adam saw no triumph on his face, only fear. "What about Zed?" He propped himself up on his elbows. "Where is he?"

"The two C17s got clear," said Eve brightly. "But with most of the strike force lost, Oldman ordered them back to Finland—"

"Zed?" Adam insisted, his voice cracking.

"He was caught in a scrum of Z. animals when they

dropped out of the sky." Zoe's voice sounded as watery as her eyes. "But it's not just him we have to worry about now . . ."

Adam didn't understand. Then he realized the nasal drone of the stealth generators had silenced. Even the regular rush of the engines sounded thin and sickly. The jet lurched, listed sharply to one side. "What's happened?"

"The stealth systems blew out and took most of the plane's electronics with them." Mr. Adlar breathed shakily. "If we hadn't gotten you out of there when we did—"

"This is Oldman." The colonel's voice crackled over the intercom like an arctic blast. "We've lost three engines. Can't get 'em restarted. We're losing altitude fast. Assume brace positions."

Adam felt sick. "We're going to crash? We got through so much and now—"

Zoe was choking back tears. "It was all for nothing."

Mr. Adlar led Adam to the couch. They sat beside Zoe and Eve and fastened their safety belts as the plane dipped downward. The whine of the last working engine built to a despairing scream.

25 POINT OF IMPACT

"My God," whispered Eve. The big TV screen was still showing the different views from the outboard CCTV, and Adam saw a toothy ridge of snow-dusted rock was looming up before them. The plane was bucking wildly on the air currents, its single engine reaching a crescendo.

"This is it!" Mr. Adlar clutched Adam's hand and shut his eyes, but Adam couldn't help but stare as the crag grew larger and larger . . .

"OMG, look!" Zoe breathed. *"Look!"*

Adam saw that Zoe was staring out through the window—then yelped as the plane heaved with some massive impact, slamming them up into the air so hard that his butt left the seat.

And then he glimpsed a mass of green scales beneath the wing.

"Zed?" Adam couldn't believe it, even when he saw the familiar tail snaking into view, dark against the glaring tundra far below. "Zed!"

"You had his back." Zoe half laughed, half sobbed with relief. "Now his back's holding us up!"

The plane shook again, and Mr. Adlar began to babble. "I don't believe it—he's trying to use his body weight to give us enough height to—"

All four cried out as the plane lurched upward once again and the jagged, icy rock scraped by just below them. Now on the screen they could see the flat, wintry wilderness surrounding the empty ghost town that marked the spot of Geneflow's underground HQ.

The ghost town that was breaking apart.

Adam was feeling so shell-shocked it took him a few moments to properly process what he was seeing. Whole tower blocks were collapsing in on themselves, violent storms of dust exploding into the air to mingle with the snow. Cracks spread wide through rows of buildings as roads were buried in an avalanche of rubble.

"What's happening?" he yelled.

Mr. Adlar stared in disbelief. "Earthquake? Or—"

Whatever his theory, it was swallowed whole by Eve's screams as the plane dipped sharply to port once again. Zed had lost his grip and was struggling to regain it.

Adam saw the thick welts gouged in his friend's head and neck, saw the mangled mess of his wings and could hardly believe they still functioned. The fierce wind was whipping blood from the wounds, and steam snorted from his nostrils as he fought doggedly to keep pace alongside the jet.

"You can do it," Adam muttered fervently. "I know you. I know you won't give up."

Zed beat his wings faster, forcing himself to fly higher. With agonizing slowness, the plane began to level out— as the plains of snow and ice came hurtling closer. Adam turned from the window and watched the nightmare action on TV; it made things seem less real somehow. He saw the rising whiteness of the ground, the concrete city still shaking itself apart on the horizon.

"Lower your heads, hold yourselves tight, be ready for impact." Oldman's terse report haunted the room for just a few moments before—

The plane grazed the surface in a spectacular explosion of snow. As Zed was snatched from sight, Adam realized no one could *ever* be ready for this.

The impact was deafening. The safety belt bit into his waist as he was jerked this way and that, unaware of anything but pain and fear. Metal screeched on rock and ice. A thunderous vibration shook at the remains of Adam's skeleton as they sped on through—what? The TVs were dead. He felt his safety belt slackening, tried to pull it tighter. *We're still going so fast . . .* The room darkened as snow piled up over the windows. Again and again, the plane struck the frozen ground. *Each time we hit, it must be slowing us down just a little,* Adam told himself. *Just hold on, just hold on, just hold on—*

Then suddenly the plane was dark and still and quiet, and someone was moaning loudly with fear, an awful panting for help. It took Adam fully half a minute to realize he was making the sound himself.

"It's all right." He felt his dad's hand on his. "We made it."

"We . . . made it?" Adam tasted blood in his mouth, guessed he'd bitten his tongue in the shake-around and gingerly moved his arms and legs, testing for damage. His ears were ringing. His neck burned with whiplash, and the whole left side of his face felt bruised. But he was in one piece.

In the faint gray light from the one emergency light in the room that hadn't failed, Adam saw that though his dad had lost his glasses and Eve had lost her breakfast down her top and Zoe's nose was bleeding, they were all still here with him. Dizzily, he took in that the plane was now angled sharply to one side; it was as if they were strapped in at the top of a steep, carpeted slide.

"How do we get out?" came Zoe's hoarse whisper.

Adam looked automatically toward the door to the

corridor beyond—but couldn't find it. The oak table and executive chairs had broken free of their fixtures and tumbled across the floor to block the exit.

"If this thing had tipped the other way," Eve said slowly, "we'd have been crushed."

"What d'you think happened to Zed?" asked Adam quietly. "Was he under the plane when it—"

"I don't know," said Mr. Adlar. "But Zed's tough. We've seen him survive worse. It's ourselves we need to worry about right now."

"So what are you sitting there for?" Chairs were pushed away from the doorway to reveal Colonel Oldman's bloodied face looking in. "Time to go."

Eve had unfastened her belt and was making her shaky way to Zoe, balancing on the sloping floor. "Did everyone make it? The pilot, the secret service guys—"

"No one but us." Oldman was still wrestling fiercely with the chairs, which seemed locked together. "And we'll die too if we don't move fast."

Familiar fear filled Adam's guts. "But we've stopped moving, haven't we?"

"There are over two hundred miles of wiring on board this plane, and our electronics shorted out. If any part of it is sparking near something flammable . . ." Oldman forced another chair clear with a heavy clatter. "Let's make survival count and *move*."

Eve and Zoe were first down the slope, shuffling down

on their backsides. Adam was about to do the same when his dad's hand grasped for his wrist.

"Ad, I can't see so good without my glasses. Can you find them for me?"

Adam looked around grimly at the wreck. "No sign. It could take us forever to find them." He squeezed his dad's hand. "I . . . I'll help you."

Together they stood, poised at the top of the tilted floor. Clinging together like tenth-rate dancers, they staggered down to join the others. Oldman hauled Zoe through the gap he'd cleared, and Eve was climbing over the chairs after her. Adam came next, helping his dad to follow. In the tense silence, his mind was full of the voice of his clone.

Just make sure you have the best life. The best life ever, for both of us.

"Dad, I have to tell you," Adam began, "when I was trying to Think-Send, I—"

"Later. Talk when we're out of here." Oldman helped Adam clamber through the gap and drop down on the other side. "Put on the thermals. Come on!"

Braced against a locker to help her balance on the sloping floor, Eve was helping Zoe dress in thermal clothing, mittens and boots. There was a big pile of similar garments and footwear on the floor; *Oldman planned ahead,* thought Adam. He quickly put on a thick quilted jacket and pants over his jeans and T-shirt and a pair of insulated gloves. It was a relief when Eve followed suit and the stench of her barf-stained top was masked by a couple of fleeces.

Once Mr. Adlar was out too, Oldman picked up some of the thermal gear and pushed it into his arms. “Put this on, and let’s go.” He tapped a large red case with his boot. “Eve, I’ll carry Zoe; can you take this first aid kit?”

“Of course.” Eve helped Zoe into Oldman’s arms. “Thank you.”

Oldman led the way through the cracked and slanted corridors at a serious pace. Eve followed with the first aid kit, and Adam helped his dad negotiate the narrow space like they were clambering through some sick carnival fun house. Finally, a shiver of freezing air spoke of an exit ahead. In fact, it was a huge V-shaped split in the side of the plane.

“The steel on either side’s razor sharp,” Oldman warned them, holding Zoe close to him as he climbed carefully out. “If you cut a vein out here, well—it’s been a long time since my field medic course, okay? So watch it.”

Adam’s gloves allowed him to swing himself down into the churned-up snow without much danger. He looked around for Zed, but there was no sign of him—only a white desert of snow, and the ruined skyline of the ghost town. Still stunned and staggered at what he’d just lived through, Adam helped his dad down onto the frozen ground.

"Come on," Oldman hollered. "Away from the plane. If she goes up now . . ."

Adam, his dad and Eve followed Oldman and Zoe as fast as they could across the snowy plain, the cold turning their ragged breaths to steam.

"All right," Oldman commanded once they were maybe three hundred yards clear of the wreck. "This ought to be far enough."

He put Zoe down, who thanked him self-consciously and turned to her mother. Eve clutched her tightly and smiled weakly at Adam and his dad. To their right, just a stone's throw away, the huge body of a Z. dactyl lay sprawled in an icy crater. Its body was a gory mess, a weighty bag of scales and flesh that had burst clean open.

I did that. Adam closed his eyes. *I mean,* we *did* . . .

"Well, if we get desperate for shelter," said Oldman, "we can always do a Luke Skywalker and hide in that thing."

Mr. Adlar squinted at the monumental spread of crimson through the snow all around. "The force of the impact destroyed it."

"And then some." Adam found he could take no pride in what he'd done. He was glad a dusting of snow now hid the worst of the mess. "D'you think all those things are dead?"

"It's likely. Deadweight, falling from fifteen thousand feet . . ."

"You did a good job, kid," Oldman muttered.

"It wasn't just me," Adam shot back.

"No, I know. Zed as well, of course. I just hope he can protect us on the ground as well as in the air—"

"I didn't mean Zed either," Adam broke in. "When I was hooked up to Think-Send, I . . . I kind of made contact with someone who was trying to stop Geneflow, and then all the buildings fell down and—"

Mr. Adlar peered at him. "Made contact with whom?"

As Adam opened his mouth, a colossal explosion ripped the VC-25A apart and lit the landscape an incandescent orange. The blast threw Adam to the ground with a wave of heat that felt hot enough to strip his skin from his back. Rolling over, he found the pale blue sky replaced by a mass of smoke and flame billowing from the plane wreck, dancing over the desolation. His dad and Oldman lay sprawled in the snow beside him, while Eve cradled Zoe in her arms, both staring wide-eyed at the wreck.

"Is everyone okay?" Mr. Adlar asked hoarsely.

"Maybe one day," muttered Zoe.

"Well, this is terrific." Oldman scrambled up, coughing. "Just in case those Russian fighter planes were having any trouble finding us, we've lit them a signal fire."

The thick drone of engines stole into the frozen stillness.

Still on the ground, Eve put an arm around Zoe. "Is that them now?"

Oldman shook his head, staring about. "Sounds like a small plane getting ready to take off."

“Geneflow’s airstrip,” Zoe realized.

“Josephs,” breathed Adam. “It’s got to be.”

“And we can’t stop her.” Oldman raised his gun up to the sky, pointing as a small white passenger aircraft climbed into the air from behind the ruins of the city. “She’ll start this whole damn thing again somewhere else, and there’s not a thing we can do—”

He broke off as the churning pillar of smoke gusting up from the jet wreck parted and a massive blur of scaly flesh scythed through high overhead. Mr. Adlar cried out in alarm, Oldman swore, Eve screamed.

Zed, Adam hoped for one desperate second.

But no, the wings were too large, the jaws long and pointed; a pterosaur was speeding from the smoke and flame like some twisted phoenix.

Adam closed his eyes, overwhelmed by frustration and fear, unable to bear the scene before him any longer. *Then . . . we didn’t stop all the Z. beasts. Josephs will escape, and this one will complete its task as ordered—and kill us all.*

26 INSTINCT TO SURVIVE

The pterosaur soared low, blotting out the sun, bearing down on Adam and his friends.

"Look! It's Keera!" Zoe screamed. "See? The scars on her wing—"

Adam felt a surge of impossible hope. "It *can't* be her! She was so sick."

"That misfiring circuitry in her head was the only thing holding back her powers to regenerate." Mr. Adlar stared up in wonder. "Her healing cycle must've kicked into overdrive."

"And she came after us . . ." The rest of Adam's words were drowned out as the Geneflow plane flew overhead—and with a screaming howl, Keera made straight for it.

"She knows who's on that plane." Zoe sounded utterly certain.

Keera was perhaps a third of the plane's size but way more maneuverable. Swooping underneath the starboard wing, she doubled back in a graceful turn and clamped her jaws down on the tail fin at the rear of the plane. Then she bent her body double and dug her talons into either side; once secured, she started scissoring through the plane's hull with those monstrous jaws.

Adam felt a shiver that went deeper than the cold as he watched Keera systematically demolish the plane, biting and tearing at its steel flanks. Suddenly flames erupted from the shattered tail section, engulfing Keera completely so that for a moment she resembled some monstrous demon wreathed in hellfire. As she let go and flapped away, her triumphant shriek all but drowned out the tortured engines.

"It's finished," said Eve, as the aircraft started going down fast. But the pilot of the plane managed to lift the craft from its fatal dive; it scraped the icy ground on its belly and cut a huge, curving swath through the snowy landscape.

"Oh, no," breathed Adam.

The plane was making like a missile straight for them.

"Run!" bellowed Oldman, half leaping, half striding through the thick snow. "Try to use my tracks."

"I can't even see them," hissed Mr. Adlar.

"That way." Adam shoved his dad after Oldman, then

turned to Eve and helped her carry Zoe. They shambled desperately through the heavy, clinging whiteness. But the plane was plowing toward them with horrible speed.

"We'll never make it!" Eve shouted.

But then Keera sailed down low, her scaly hide blackened by the flames, and slammed her entire body into the front end of the plane. The aircraft was sent scraping away from Adam's group and toward the blazing remains of the VC-25A. The snow piled up around it, finally halting its horrible progress a short distance from the first wreck. The gusting wind had changed direction too, cloaking both planes in dark, stinking smoke as if trying to draw a veil over the whole sorry scene.

Silently, Keera flapped away without a backward look, to land with a crump and clatter of folding wings a few yards from where Adam, Zoe and Eve cowered together. She sat, heaving for breath, her eyes dark and unfathomable. And while Oldman and Mr. Adlar backed away in frightened wonder, Zoe pushed herself through the snow toward her.

"Zoe, no!" Eve began.

"It's all right," Zoe insisted. "She's different, but . . . she doesn't want to hurt us. I know it." She pulled off her mitts and pressed her thick-fingered hands against the pterosaur's scaly flank. She made soft cooing noises that Keera seemed to echo, almost lost beneath the wind's breath.

Adam retreated to his dad, pressed himself up against

him for comfort. But Oldman, it seemed, was more concerned with the downed plane, which lay half hidden by the billowing curtain of smoke. "I need to check that wreck for survivors," he announced. "We need Geneflow staff alive for prosecution. If the flames spread from our plane, no one inside will stand a chance."

"But it could explode at any moment," Eve protested. "You're the one who told us that if any wiring sparks near the fuel tanks—"

"Do as I say, not as I do. And stay well back."

He trudged past Zoe and Keera, making for the half-buried plane.

"She didn't come here for revenge," Zoe said distantly. "Didn't even come to help us." She turned to Adam. "She came because we made her free—and the only way to be sure she can *stay* free is—"

"Is to kill Josephs," Adam concluded.

Zoe nodded slowly, pressed her head against Keera's side. "I think . . . after all she's gone through . . . she just needs to be sure."

Adam nodded too, a mess of emotions. "I think we all do." Why should he be surprised by Keera's savagery? Hunger, pain, the hunt, the kill . . . Like Zed, she might know plenty more, but he supposed these were the only things she really understood.

Eve watched Oldman draw closer to the Geneflow plane wreck. "I guess he needs Geneflow personnel as witnesses if he's going to put the world straight."

"Or if he wants to put them to work for the US military," said Mr. Adlar cynically.

But then a series of clangs—something bone-hard striking metal—stopped Oldman in his tracks. Adam looked nervously at his dad. The clangs were followed by a sharp, rending scrape.

Then Oldman jumped backward and slipped, yelling out in surprise as a gargantuan, scaly hulk leaped out through the smoke and thumped down in front of the plane.

"Zed!" Stunned, Adam stared at his friend. "Zed, is it . . . are you . . . ?"

Zoe turned to him, her grin wide and full. "I *knew* he couldn't be dead!"

Adam couldn't tear his eyes away. "I really thought this time we'd lost him."

But his delight was tempered by Zed's condition. The beast was swaying on bloodied legs, his head and neck a mass of deep welts and bites. One eye was a swollen mess, but the other eye glinted bright in the flames. He was clutching a large, misshapen bundle in his arms, holding it to his chest like it was treasure. As the wind cleared the smoke further, Adam realized Zed's haul appeared to be a half-dozen blood-soaked bodies.

"Back," Zed said.

"Oh, yes, you had our backs, all right . . ." Adam charged toward his friend, tripping and tumbling across the snow.

"No, Ad," his dad bellowed. "You heard Oldman—that wreck could go up any moment!"

Adam couldn't stop himself. He ran past Oldman, all the way up to Zed, and pressed himself against the terrifying animal's warm, heaving flank. "Thank you," he whispered. "Just . . . thanks. Without you . . ."

"Back," Zed said again, his voice a splintered growl.

Adam realized Zed might be warning him away. Looking up at Zed uncertainly, he retreated to join Oldman. "You . . . you're all right, aren't you?"

Oldman was staring at the grisly bundle of bodies Zed was holding. "Those people. Are they alive?"

"Others dead. These ones . . . live."

"So *that* was the scraping noise," Oldman mumbled. "He opened the plane like a tin of sardines and fished out the live ones."

"But look at them." Adam stared, repulsed but fascinated by the tough scales that patterned the bodies' dark green skin.

"This is what you meant by hybrids?" Oldman murmured.

Adam nodded. "Like the clone of my dad . . . like Zoe and me."

"I guess they all turned reptile to be ready to start their new world," said Oldman. "Prematurely, let's hope."

Zed strode past them both, away from the plane wrecks, his badly mauled tail dragging through the snow.

Adam and Oldman hurried after him as Zed dumped the grisly pile of victims in front of Keera and Zoe.

Eve and Mr. Adlar came over to see. A grotesque, powerful-looking creature, half woman, half reptile, was sprawled on top of the pile, both legs bloody and clearly pulverized, her breath fast and shallow.

Adam's heart twisted as he recognized the distorted features. "Josephs."

Mr. Adlar peered down at her myopically. "What has she done to herself?"

"Stage one of her grand design," said Adam. "She did that to you too."

A low, menacing noise started up somewhere in Keera's chest, and Zoe tried to shush her. Zed sank to his haunches in the snow and watched as Oldman, Eve and Mr. Adlar tried to separate the gruesome tangle of bodies, laying them out straight. Adam hunkered down beside Zed and tried rubbing snow into one of the deeper gashes in the scaly neck. But when the beast flinched and growled, Adam took the hint. *Guess I'll leave dino first aid to the experts.*

"Where . . . ?" Josephs stirred and coughed, staining her chin with blood. "Where am I?"

"In your own backyard," snapped Mr. Adlar. "The animal you created and tried to kill brought you down."

"No, where am *I*? Me . . . the me before . . ." She brushed her fingers against her scaly cheek. "Before this?"

Oldman glanced back at the wreck of the Geneflow plane. "If she was in there with you, she's dead."

Josephs's eyes closed. Her breathing grew more erratic.

"We're going to need the mother of all first aid kits," Eve muttered.

Adam saw the red case lying on its side in the snow between them and the wreck. Since there was nothing he could do for Zed, he ran over, braving the fierce heat of the flames to retrieve it. *How many times have I dreamed of Josephs lying beaten at last? Never looking like that, but even so . . .* Adam had always imagined he'd feel awesomely triumphant. Instead, he found he felt nothing but a cold, weary relief.

He set the first aid box down beside Oldman, who tore it open. He grabbed a loaded syringe from the kit with bloody fingers and jabbed it into Josephs's shoulder. "Now, come on, Samantha. I can fix you up. But you need to tell us about your accomplices. The other bases you got."

Josephs's eyes flickered open as the drug went to work. She looked down at her crushed legs and groaned, shaking her head.

"Not quite perfection, is it?" Zoe hissed spitefully. "Prisoner of your own 'unfortunate' body now. Doesn't look like you made it quite tough enough."

Eve shook her head. "Don't gloat, Zoe."

"You want me to feel sorry for her?" Zoe looked stung. "Josephs deserves it! After all she's done . . . the blood on her hands, she deserves to be dead."

"Maybe." Oldman unzipped Josephs's coat to reveal a grisly open wound in her ribs. Adam felt sick, but the colonel calmly tore a large field dressing from its wrapper and straightened the airtight material.

Zed turned away, apparently uninterested, pressing his raw body into the soothing snow.

"Come on, Josephs, breathe out for me." As she did so, Oldman placed the wrapper over the wound. "Eve, can you apply the dressing?"

Keera made another chittering noise. "Let her die," Zoe whispered, as if translating.

"She's got to live," said Oldman, "so she can be put on trial."

Mr. Adlar nodded. "The whole world will hear the truth at last, straight from her mouth."

At the sound of Mr. Adlar's voice, Josephs's dark eyes seemed to focus. "You. I guessed it would be you." She looked between him and Adam. "I'd already ordered evacuation when your planes were detected. Thought my creations would deal with you . . ."

"We stopped them." Mr. Adlar frowned. "Why were you evacuating? What brought down the city?"

"Our atomic reactor . . . and *you.*" Josephs started to shiver. "Your clone barricaded himself inside with the son I permitted him . . . forced the reactor core into meltdown. The buildup of heat in the containment units produced a massive steam explosion deep underground, destroyed the whole base."

Oldman looked at Mr. Adlar. "Making this whole area radioactive?"

"The bedrock below us will have absorbed a lot of it," Eve volunteered. Mr. Adlar nodded uncertainly.

But Adam was jolted from his fears as Josephs looked up at him, eyes narrowed. "All this," she whispered. "Because of *him*."

"Me?" Adam's spine didn't just tingle; it almost shook itself apart. *You made Dad see what he'd become,* his clone had said.

Made him decide what he had to do about that.

"Oh, Dad." Adam turned to his father. "I was trying to tell you, back on the plane—me and that clone of me, in the Think-Send world, we *connected.* He helped me bring down the dinosaurs, and he"—he swallowed as fresh tears threatened to form—"he knew he was going to die. He—*I*—must've been so afraid, but still he helped us."

"Easy, Ad," his dad breathed.

"I don't understand." Josephs moaned with pain as Eve tightened the bandage around her. Already the thick white material was turning scarlet. "He'd been conditioned . . . He wanted what Geneflow wanted . . ." She grimaced. "How could seeing Adam again break through that conditioning?"

"You know so much, Sam," Mr. Adlar said quietly, "but I doubt if you could ever understand that."

"I made another Adam . . . made him stronger, better

than before . . ." Her voice was dwindling to a croaking whisper. "The two of you could've lived together in a better world. A world that makes sense."

"Whatever you did to me in there . . . I'd never share your idea of what makes sense." Mr. Adlar's lip curled. "You look at us like we're walking, talking sacks of chemicals, but we're not. We're *people.* We're put here by chance, we're shaped by happenstance, we blunder through life the best way we can. It's not the design that makes us better—it's that journey."

"Sentimental bull . . . ," Josephs sneered, a trickle of blood escaping her lips.

"You call that bull?" Eve shook her head as she applied a further dressing to the gory chest wound. "You're insane."

Josephs coughed, and blood dribbled from her mouth. "What's insane . . . is to sacrifice yourself . . . for a world that's already on the scrap heap."

"All right, enough," said Oldman impatiently. "Josephs, I need to know more on your accomplices, your methods, the scientists you kidnapped . . ."

But then a whooshing roar of engines thundered overhead. Adam looked up to see what looked like three pencil leads sketching vapor trails across the sky. Zed stirred uneasily, and Keera bucked and screeched, almost knocking Zoe over.

"Fighter jets." Oldman saw Josephs close her eyes and

shook her awake. "Hear that? The Russian military's on its way. But I can protect you, see that you get a fair trial, if you only—"

"You can't judge me . . ." She shook her head, dark eyes shining. "You just better hope . . . my clones . . . don't come looking . . ."

"They're dead," said Adam. "They've got to be."

Josephs opened her mouth as if to say something more. But only thick, glottal noises came out as her breath began to bubble in the back of her throat. Her eyes began to flicker shut.

The MiGs swept back in earsplitting formation overhead.

"Ground forces will be here soon," Oldman muttered. "Josephs! Josephs, stay with me!"

But she was unconscious now, breathing shallowly. Though her features were alien and unsettling, she looked weirdly peaceful.

"I . . . guess it's a good thing we'll be picked up soon," Eve said, looking up at the trails in the sky. "We won't last long in these conditions, and with the risk of radiation . . ."

Adam nodded, turned to the mountain of rubble that marked the Geneflow base like some chaotic gravestone and wondered what trace remained of two lives deep beneath. A father and his boy who had never truly lived, but who might just have saved the world for untold billions who would.

Then he went to his dad and hugged him close. He saw that Zed, despite his battle scars, was watching the skies intently. But for Adam, right now, in this desolate backwater, the Russian troops weren't the enemy—they were the cavalry.

"We're losing Josephs," Oldman said bitterly. "All that she knows . . . it'll die with her."

"Maybe not," said Zoe. "I don't know who those other survivors are, but that man there is called Thierry."

Adam looked over to find her pointing to a balding hybrid with a wispy gray beard. "Yeah—he reported to Josephs. He'll know everything about their plan."

Oldman inspected Thierry, feeling for a pulse. "I don't know what's normal for your average alligator man. But aside from this head wound, he doesn't seem too badly hurt."

"Josephs, on the other hand . . ." Mr. Adlar looked down at the architect of a world that would never be, dead now in her own congealing blood. "It's over."

For a few seconds, no one moved or spoke. Then suddenly, Keera jerked into life and shook out the vast, leathery sails of her wings. She was scarred and battered, but still so strong. As she stood there, the last of her kind, there was something in her that was almost majestic. She looked over at Adam, eyes bright but unreadable. Then she turned toward Zoe, and lowered her head a little.

"She's going," Zoe murmured.

There was no parting cry, no hesitation, not even a backward glance. With Josephs dead, Keera's hard-won freedom was hers to take. She took a few steps and launched herself into the sky.

Good-bye, thought Adam, his mind full of all they had shared these last days.

He saw that Zoe was crying; her mum came to comfort her. "It's okay, love. She'll be all right out there."

"Yeah," Zoe said quietly. "She will be, now."

Zed broke the peace first, growling suddenly as if in warning. Alerted, Oldman pointed up at some black specks in the sky. "Russian military helicopters incoming!"

"Here we go, then. Prisoners of war. This'll be original." Eve looked up at Mr. Adlar and pressed her forehead against his chest. "Jeez, what a morning!"

"You could say that." He put an arm around her. "Colonel Oldman, what do you think will happen? If the president is going to deny this mission took place—"

"We'll be fine," he said firmly. "There's proof that Geneflow was behind the whole scam all around us. And old Doc Marrs packs some weight at the UN—he'll be pulling strings for us." He looked down at the sleeping Thierry. "No one can deny we came up with the goods today. The Russians won't hurt us—they need to talk with us. And I've got plenty to say."

Yeah, thought Adam. *But you can leave Zed right out of it.* Adam crossed to join the battered dinosaur. Zed shifted a little as he approached, raised his head from the snow.

"You've got to split," Adam told him. "There are more soldiers coming."

Zed stared at him with his one good eye, but said nothing.

"They . . . they won't hurt me," said Adam with something that at least approached conviction, "but they'll try to hurt you, or capture you or worse." He pressed his hand against Zed's bleeding face. "So, you have to go."

Zed snorted softly. "Hurts."

"I know it does." Adam nodded. "It must. With all you've been through, I don't know how you're still standing. But even if you just hide out round here for a bit, till you do your super-healing thing—"

"Go. *Hurts.*"

Adam took his hand away, feeling helpless. "Dad, is there anything in the first aid kit we could—"

"Hey, Ad?" Zoe called. "I . . . don't think Zed means that kind of hurt."

"Oh." Adam watched as the creature slowly heaved himself up. "I . . . I get you, Zed." He lowered his voice. "But I don't want anyone else to get you. You're like Keera—you need to be free. And these soldiers . . . or Oldman, even . . . they might try and use me to capture you."

"Not hurt . . . us," Zed snarled. "Never."

"We can't always win, Zed. No one can." Adam felt cut up inside. "You've got to promise me you'll go now and never come back for me. Never." He looked up helplessly at the beast staring down at him. "Do you even know what a promise is?"

Zed cocked his head as if quizzical. "Got . . . your back?"

"Yeah, that was a promise." Adam tried to force a smile. "And you kept it. You helped to land our plane, saved our lives. Now it's my turn to save yours—by making sure you go, and *stay* gone." He chewed his lip furiously to stop the tears. "Don't you see? That's the only way I'll know for sure you'll be okay—if you leave me and don't ever come back."

The hum of the helicopters was growing larger, stealing into the blue expanse of the sky as if claiming ownership. The sound seemed to break whatever spell had held Zed motionless. Without another word, he turned and pounded unsteadily away.

Then he leaped through the smoke still pouring from the blazing jet and disappeared from Adam's sight.

Dimly, Adam felt fingers take his own; he saw that Eve had helped Zoe over to join him.

"How about that?" she muttered, tears drying now on her own face. "Boy meets dinosaur, boy falls in love with dinosaur, dinosaur has to leave . . . The same old story, huh?"

"Shut up." Angrily, Adam tried to pull his hand away. But Zoe's grip was too tight, and the understanding in her eyes too tender. He took a deep breath and forced a smile. "Shut up," he said again, more softly this time. "It's a *great* story." He stared on into the wide blue heavens, picturing Keera and Zed as they began their journeys to freedom.

Stay safe, guys, he thought.

The drone of the copters grew louder still as they dropped out of the sky, whipping up the snow into a bitter wind. Well-armed black-clad troops started fast-roping down to confront the misfit group invading their country—little dreaming that those misfits had most likely saved it.

Zoe looked at him. "The next few days are going to be tough."

"I reckon we've evolved thick enough skins to take it," said Adam.

Mr. Adlar nodded. "The truth—however incredible—will always get out in the end."

And we'll get out too, Adam told himself firmly. *Ready to start again.*

He looked at Zoe. "What's Russian for 'extra-large pepperoni pizza, please'?"

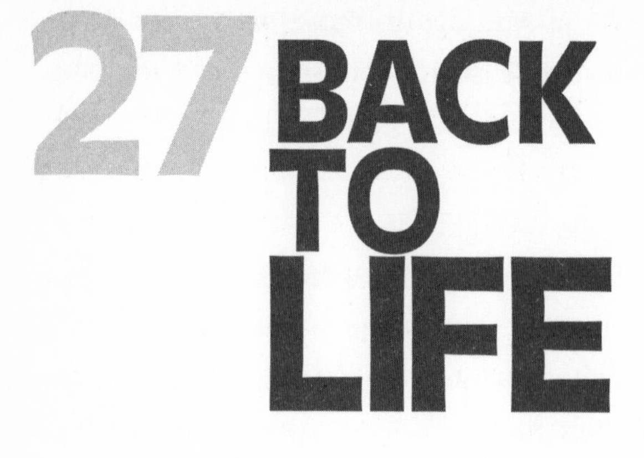

27 BACK TO LIFE

One month later, Adam sat with his dad in Princes Street Gardens, a swathe of peaceful green in the center of Edinburgh. From his bench, he could contemplate the blackened sandstone splendor of the city and the colorful parkland that endured alongside it, each enhancing the other's appeal. For centuries, the gardens had been overlooked by Edinburgh Castle—before Geneflow's clone of Zed had smashed the old building to rubble.

Happily, the castle was being rebuilt. For now, a cocoon of ugly scaffolding squatted on the Mound—but one day the stonework behind it would break free to stand proud again.

Adam sighed. His own cocoon was harder to spot, but he knew he'd wrapped it tight around himself this last year. To be caught up in something so big and so frightening . . . it had meant he'd shied away from real life. Become a loner.

Ironically, it was the seven days he'd spent under house arrest by the Russian government that had seen the first cracks in the chrysalis appear.

The world's press and TV had gone crazy for the story of how the world had been saved from disaster by such a small and unlikely band. And the role of the two children, the average boy from Scotland and the lovely, crippled girl from Down Under—and their special bond with monsters—had caught the imagination of practically everyone on the planet. And once Oldman's story and motives had checked out and the nations of the world had taken the first steps back to a lasting peace, the Adlars, Eve and Zoe had been released into a media storm.

Of the four of them, Adam had actually welcomed the attention most. He'd relished talking about the stuff he'd imagined no one would ever believe. Magazine interviews, TV and radio shows, live streaming broadcasts, he'd done them all—chiefly to rid himself of all the baggage he'd been heaving around and hiding behind.

Soon he'd be seeing Zoe again, and his fellow survivors from Raptor Island too. Like him, and like most of the kidnapped scientists who'd made it aboveground before Josephs's reactor blew apart, they were going to give evidence against Geneflow in what would surely be one of the biggest criminal trials in history. Josephs might be dead, but subordinates like Thierry had pulled through. Powerless now, trapped in their freakish forms and with the world baying for their blood, they had cut a deal with the world's authorities—providing details of Geneflow's hidden bases and secret benefactors around the globe in exchange for a guarantee that death sentences would not be passed.

Finally, when the trial was over and the glaring eye of the world had moved elsewhere, the last scraps of old Adam's cocoon were gone, and a new Adam finally emerged.

Z. Adam, he thought wryly.

That was the plan, anyway.

But what exactly do Z. Adams do?

"Ahhh." His dad sat beside him on the bench, sighed contentedly. "To feel the sun on your skin and know you have nothing to do today—this is officially the life."

Adam smiled. The publicity had resulted in real corporate interest in developing Ultra-Reality as a major game system at last, and his dad was hot property.

"I guess you could say it's the life," Adam agreed. "But is it the best life?"

"My son, the philosopher," teased his dad.

"Seriously," Adam protested. "I think I need to have the best life ever. After all, how many people can say they sacrificed themselves to save the world and lived to talk about it?" He felt a stroke of sadness for the different him, trapped in the Geneflow base, waiting for the reactor to run wild. "Yeah . . . I've got to live enough for *two.* I've got to live—"

"The *Z.* life?"

"Right," Adam agreed. "A life at its zenith."

Mr. Adlar smiled. "We've reached our highest point through surviving our lowest. I suppose high and low will always chase each other."

Adam smiled. "Now you're at it. My *dad,* the philosopher."

"Sorry." Mr. Adlar looked at him and grinned. "If you've got to live enough for two, what would you say to a couple of ice creams right now, followed by a couple of pizzas from Brown's?"

"I'd say yum," Adam decided. "That's my kind of philosophy."

As he and his dad set off toward the ice cream stand, for a moment the sun seemed to flicker. Adam felt a shadow pass over him. He looked up. But there were no blurred outlines in the sky, and no distant, bestial cries reached his ears.

"What's up?" asked his dad.

"Oh . . . nothing." *Imagination, I suppose,* Adam thought. It was kind of comforting to think that Zed or Keera might still watch over him in the years to come—but he knew it was incredibly selfish of him too. He had to hope the Z. beasts would find some greater purpose on their journeys, a way to be as happy as two fantastical animals caught out of time could ever be.

We've all won our freedom. And I guess in the end, we'll figure out what to do with it.

He looked up at the wide, open blue that stretched high above the park and sandstone, that reached around the world.

The sky's the limit.